THE TEXAS GUN

Lew Troop, bronc stomper and saddle tramp from Texas, drifted on to the homestead of Fern Bergstrom with the intention of just passing through. But he fell under Fern's fiery spell and went to work for her as a hired hand. Then the cattlemen decided that the range wasn't big enough for them and a homestead, and they took aim at Lew. That was their mistake. Lew Troop owned a temper and a gun that were enough to tear the cattle country apart.

THE TEXAS GUN

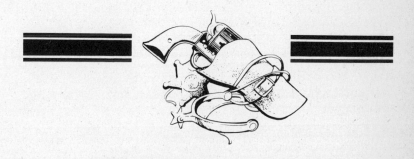

Leslie Ernenwein

ATLANTIC LARGE PRINT
Chivers Press, Bath, England.
John Curley & Associates Inc.,
South Yarmouth, Mass., USA.

Library of Congress Cataloging in Publication Data

Ernenwein, Leslie.
  The Texas gun.

  (Atlantic large print)
  1. Large type books.   I. Title.
  [PS3555.R58T4 1986]   813'.54   85–14930
  ISBN 0–89340–951–0 (Curley: lg. print)

British Library Cataloguing in Publication Data

Ernenwein, Leslie
  The Texas gun.—Large print ed.—(Atlantic
  large print)
  I. Title
  813'.52[F]   PS3555.R5/

  ISBN 0–7451–9104–5

This Large Print edition is published by Chivers Press, England, and
John Curley & Associates, Inc, U.S.A. 1986

Published by arrangement with Donald MacCampbell, Inc

U.K. Hardback ISBN 0 7451 9104 5
U.S.A. Softback ISBN 0 89340 951 0

THE TEXAS GUN

CHAPTER ONE

Lew Troop came off the ridge trail at noon, a lean, long-shanked man riding with a drifter's indolence. If he appeared older than his twenty-seven years it was because sun and wind had etched their ancient symbols in his face, for he wasn't one to worry, this Lew Troop. Possessing no more worldly goods than those in the blanket roll behind his saddle, he was free as a migratory mallard.

A pleasant sense of that freedom—of going yonderly—was in Troop now as he contemplated the scatter of corrals and sheds, bunkhouse, blacksmith shop, and commissary that flanked the big log house at Slash C headquarters. It occurred to him that Dade Chastain, who owned all this, wasn't free. Dade couldn't high-tail for the tules when he got an itchy foot; he couldn't pull his picket pin and take off like a blanket squaw hunting a hogan in the hills. Dade Chastain owned so much that he was trapped by his possessions. Even though he had no wife to nag him or children to provide for, Chastain lived a treadmill life.

A dollar-grabbing fool, Troop thought. He had worked for some greedy galoots in the past ten years, but none who could hold a smoking lantern to Dade Chastain.

It was warm today, drowsy warm, with autumn haze forming a fragile blue banner all across Cathedral Basin. Winter seemed far away, but Lew Troop knew different. The aspens had turned yellow, and mountain ponies were making coat. This was November—'Moon of Falling Leaves,' the Indians called it. One of these mornings there'd be snow on the ground and a cold wind prowling the high pines.

Troop shivered, just thinking about it. The Big Die in Texas had occurred thirteen years ago, but the tragedy of that long and bitter winter had marked him so that he feared snow as most men feared the plague.

'We'll be down on the desert by this time next week,' Troop told his horse, a strong-muscled *grulla*, so called because of its bluish-gray color. 'No goddamn snowballs for us.'

Riding on into the Slash C yard, Troop grinned a wordless greeting to Monk Monroe and Oak Creek Kirby, who were dehorning a herd bull in the crowding corral. Their blood-sprayed faces showed more surprise than friendliness, and so did the high-beaked face of Dade Chastain, who peered at him from the front gallery. They'd be curious to know why he wasn't at the Sun Dance Hills horse camp

2

having his britches bounced by a hump-backed bronc.

Chastain didn't wait for him to come across the yard. The dark and gaunt and perpetually frowning cowman called, 'What you doing here at this time of day?'

'Stopped by to collect my wages,' Troop said, not dismounting.

Most men would have invited a rider to get down and rest his saddle as a matter of cow-country custom. But not Chastain. Dade paid a man to work, and he couldn't abide daylight dawdling. He said sourly, 'This ain't payday.'

'It is for me,' Troop announced.

Chastain squinted at him for a full moment before demanding, 'You mean you're quitting?'

Troop nodded.

'Why?'

'Well, if a man has to have a reason, I'd say that three months in one horse camp is aplenty.'

'Three months! Why, that ain't scarcely time for a man to learn his way around an outfit. You and Joe Maffitt have a fuss?'

Troop shook his head. 'Just need a change, is all.'

'Meaning you want a woman,' Chastain said censuringly. 'Well, I don't cotton to men traipsing off to town in the middle of the

3

week, but I'll advance half your wages so you can go sniff some parlor-house perfumery in Signal. Be back in two days. We're starting the Rimrock gather day after tomorrow.'

'No,' Troop said. 'I need a change of scenery.'

Chastain stared at him with plain disbelief in his flinty blue eyes. 'You mean you'd quit a high-paying job just to take a look-see over the hill?'

There was a commotion in the corral. The released bull shook its blood-spurting horn stubs and charged in blind, bellowing fury. Troop watched Monk and Oak Creek climb the fence, then he said, 'Three months in one place is long enough.'

'But that's no fit reason to quit when I'm short-handed,' Chastain objected. 'There's a thousand head of cattle to be brought off the Rimrock and moved to winter range. A job that needs doing before we get a snow-storm.'

He waited for some sign from Troop, and getting none, added scowlingly, 'I'll pay the same wages you been getting—bronc-stomper wages.'

Troop took out his Durham sack and fashioned a cigarette. Chastain, he supposed, just couldn't understand why a man might be unwilling to freeze his rump all winter for high wages. It wouldn't make sense to Dade, who owned the biggest ranch in Cathedral Basin and had more money than he'd ever need, yet kept grabbing for more. That was a thing that puzzled Lew Troop. What made a man want so much?

'You won't find many outfits paying that kind of money for winter riding,' Chastain said. He seldom smiled, and he didn't now, but his voice lost some of its gritty arrogance as he added, 'You could save up a real nice stake, come spring.'

'Shouldn't wonder,' Troop mused, exhaling a long drag of smoke. Then he said, 'Look, Chastain. I don't like snowballs. I'm heading south tomorrow morning, and I want my wages.'

Anger darkened Chastain's russet cheeks so that his blue eyes seemed bleached and colorless. 'Drifters!' he scoffed, smearing the word with contempt. 'You're all cut from the same sorry pattern. Shiftless saddle tramps making horse tracks all over hell!'

'That's me,' Troop admitted with a grin. 'Foot-loose and fancy free. Come and go as I please.'

'A smart aleck that'll end up a bare-assed bum,' predicted Chastain. 'I've seen your kind before, and I never knowed one that didn't sell his saddle before he was fifty.'

'Shouldn't wonder,' Troop agreed, holding

5

out his hand. 'Fork over, friend, so's I can start making me some fresh horse tracks.'

Chastain drew a money pouch from his hip pocket, loosened its drawstrings, and took out a wad of folded bills. Watching Dade count out his wages, Troop observed the man's big-knuckled fingers and dirt-encrusted nails. A penniless cowpoke's hands would look no worse, nor would he thumb a dollar bill with more caution.

'You owe the commissary for three dollars' worth of tobacco and a pair of gloves,' Chastain muttered. He counted the exact amount with a reluctant regard for each two-bit piece, saying, 'Now git off my land and be quick about it.'

'You wouldn't rush me, would you?' Troop asked, pocketing the money.

'Go on, and when you leave Cathedral Basin don't come back!'

'Do you own it all?' Troop inquired with the wide-eyed look of a country boy on his first trip to town. 'The whole basin?'

'No, but I run it!' Chastain shouted.

Lew Troop bowed with exaggerated politeness. He said solemnly, 'Good-by, God,' and tipped his hat. When he passed Monroe and Kirby roosting on the corral fence, he called, 'So long, angels.'

'What you mean angels?' Monk

demanded.

'Well, you work for God, don't you?' Troop said.

Riding on out of the yard, he loosed a hoot of derisive laughter.

Dade Chastain strode toward the corral, shouted, 'Quit your goddamn gawking and git to work!'

And now, observing the cook, who stood empty-handed in the commissary doorway, Chastain demanded, 'Why ain't you out there greasing them chuck-wagon wheels like I told you?'

The cook hurried toward the wagon shed, wiping his hands on a flour-sack apron. Monroe and Kirby climbed hastily into saddle and began hazing the dehorned bull out of the crowding corral.

'One of you loafers ride up to the horse camp and tell Maffitt to be here tomorrow night with his bed roll,' Chastain commanded.

Then, as an odd croaking sounded overhead, Chastain glimpsed a flight of geese that formed a widespread V against the sky. 'More bums heading south,' he muttered disgustedly.

CHAPTER TWO

Afternoon's sun was casting long shadows when Lew Troop followed a deep-grooved trail down Cemetery Slope and glanced at the stone-piled mound that had given the place its name. According to bunkhouse gossip, the grave contained the bones of a Curly Bill renegade who'd been buried here soon after the wild bunch sacked Matamoras. Nearby, partly covered by drifting dust, were rusty wheel rims, a smoke-blackened axle, and two hubs—all that remained of what had been a high-wheeled Mexican *carreta*. The bandits, Troop reflected, must have transported heavy loot to use so ponderous and slow-moving a conveyance.

Afterward, crossing the Free Strip flats, Troop passed an abandoned cabin with its broken fence and weed-grown remnants of a garden. The cabin's open door revealed a rammed earth floor littered by cow droppings. This, he recalled, was Swede Borgstrom's place.

'The nester who owned the Jersey cow,' Troop mused.

Swede Borgstrom was dead now. He had stuck it out on the Free Strip longer than anyone else, and had got himself killed in a gun fight. But he was best remembered for being the man who'd brought a Jersey heifer into the country. An odd thing to be famous for, Troop reflected. Thinking of other abandoned shacks like this, he wondered what stubborn urge impelled men to buck a big outfit like Slash C. All they stood to win was a frugal living and a lifetime of tedious toil, most of it on foot. Yet the sodbusters risked their lives to gain a toe hold in a game that was invariably rigged against them. A game they never won. Such men, he reckoned, must be addlebrained at birth.

When Troop came to the stage road he followed it to Canteen Creek and allowed his horse to halt midway across the shallow stream. 'Drink if you like,' he told the grulla gelding. 'I'll take mine in town—from a bottle.'

A grin rutted Troop's angular face as he thought how long a time it had been since he'd bellied up to a bar, or bucked the tiger, or seen a flirty-eyed female. Five straight weeks without coming to town. Better than thirty days of riding the rough string with only mean-tempered Joe Maffitt for company. It was enough to give a man the running fits.

I'll celebrate in Signal tonight and take the south trail in the morning, Troop thought. He wondered if Belle Smith was still dancing her heels off at the Bon Ton. She had treated him like kinfolk from Texas the last time he was in town. Troop grinned, thinking how it would be to have her in his arms again. Belle was a lot of woman and one who savvied what a lone man needed to cheer him up.

There was another one at the Bon Ton who'd be real good company—a big blonde named Grace. 'Maybe I'll give 'em both a whirl,' Troop reflected.

He was like that, sitting there asaddle without a worry in the world, when he saw the sorrel-haired woman.

It was an odd thing. Lew Troop was remotely aware of the team and a tarp-covered wagon. But all he really saw was the woman with sunlit sorrel hair and eyes that were blue, or gray, or green. She sat alone on the wagon's spring seat, holding a line in each slender up-palmed hand; sat poised as a queen might sit a royal coach.

That's how she looked to Lew Troop. Like a full-blooded, prideful queen. Perhaps it was because he hadn't seen a woman for so long, or because, at this first glance, she seemed to possess everything a man wanted to see in a woman. It fairly took his breath away just to look at her.

She drove up to the creek, not glancing at

Troop until the team stopped to drink. Then, as if his presence annoyed her, she asked, 'Is this the first time you ever saw a woman drive a wagon?'

'No, ma'am,' Troop said.

'Then why are you staring?' she demanded. Her left hand lifted to explore the buttoned blouse above the swell of her breasts, and she asked, 'Am I unbuttoned someplace?'

'No, ma'am,' Troop said again.

In all his foot-loose wandering he had never met a woman like her. She could look a man in the eye; could size him up with frank interest, and yet not seem brazen. Her appraising glance traveled from his sweat-stained Texas hat to the toes of his brush-scabbed boots, not missing the Walker Model Colt he wore in a half-breed holster.

'A warm day for this time of year,' he offered.

She nodded, not speaking for a moment as her gaze shifted to scan the west side of the creek. And in this interval Troop decided that her eyes were blue. Blue and warm as a desert sky. She was not more than twenty-five or -six, he reckoned, and medium tall with womanly contours that a tan blouse and green corduroy skirt couldn't conceal.

'Can you direct me to the Borgstrom homestead?' she asked.

Her voice was low and throaty. Like singing, Troop thought. A rich mellow voice with a hint of sadness in it; a voice that seemed in perfect harmony with her wide eyes and mobile, full-lipped mouth and high-boned cheeks; with her womanliness.

'Take the first right fork of the road,' Troop directed, wondering why she should want to go there. 'You figuring to stay at Borgstrom's place tonight?'

She nodded. A slow smile curved her lips and she said, 'Every night from now on. I own it.'

'You own it!'

'Gus Borgstrom was my father,' she said quietly.

Swede's daughter. It scarcely seemed possible. How could a man like Swede Borgstrom sire such a woman?

She said, 'It was his intention to get a farm started while I helped by teaching school in Texas. He was a good man, my father. A God-fearing man who wanted a home in Arizona Territory. It was his dream.'

She shrugged, and the sadness of her voice was mirrored in her eyes when she added, 'They told me in Signal that my father turned to drink and gambling—that he was killed in an argument over cards.'

'So I heard,' Troop said. He wondered if

12

they had told her the rest of it; how the Slash C headquarters crew hounded her father until he finally took a job in town, leaving his sorry shack to cattle and kangaroo rats. Or if they had explained to her that Dade Chastain would make life miserable for anyone who settled on the homestead strip that ran between his range and Canteen Creek—the long flat-bottomed valley they called the Free Strip. That was a joke. For Chastain had sworn that no god-damn plow jockey would ever harvest a crop there, and none ever had.

'Did they tell you about the other trouble?' Troop asked.

She nodded. 'A wood peddler named Joe Shedrow tried to frighten me, saying that Dade Chastain would not allow homesteaders near his range. And Sheriff Eggleston said I'd be wasting my time, because the land was not fit for raising crops. But I laughed at them. It's my place and I shall live there.'

Then she asked abruptly, 'Are you a Slash C rider?'

'No, ma'am,' Troop said, glad that he'd had no part in forcing Swede off his place. 'I'm just sort of drifting through.' Remembering his manners, he announced, 'Name of Troop—Lew Troop.'

She acknowledged that courtesy by saying, 'And I'm Fern Borgstrom.'

13

The quiet pride of her, the dignity and self-assurance, reminded Troop of a poem he'd once read; something about a Viking's daughter. That struck him as being odd, for Swede Borgstrom had been no Viking. Not at the last. He'd been a beaten, booze-guzzling nester scared off his land; a fumbling, confused sodbuster doing odd jobs in town for his betters. Like all the others who'd built their sorry shacks on Free Strip grass. Well, not exactly like the others, for Borgstrom had held his ground against Slash C for almost a year.

Troop told her that. He said, 'No one else ever held out so long against Chastain.'

But that didn't seem to impress her. She sighed, and murmured, 'It was his dream.'

She came down off the wagon. She knelt there beside the road and scooped up a handful of powdery soil and let it trickle slowly through her fingers. Lew Troop had seen men do that; men with a liking for the land. But never a woman.

'It is good,' she said, gently smiling.

Troop watched her get back on the wagon, seeing how gracefully her supple body moved; how slanting sunlight burnished her braided, high-coiled hair. She picked up the lines and said, 'I must be going.'

'Me too,' Troop said.

14

'A long journey?'

He shrugged, having no definite goal beyond Signal. 'Somewhere south,' he said, and remembering that the cabin had been befouled by cows using it for shelter, he warned, 'That place will have to be mucked out before you move in.'

'I'll muck it,' she said.

Troop looked into her eyes and marveled at their blue depth, and he thought, A man could drown in them. He grinned, thinking how warm and pleasant an end that would be, just so her woman's arms were around him. It made a man itch just to look at her.

He said, 'I'd be glad to give you a hand in mucking out that cabin.'

'I suppose you would,' she murmured, as if this was an old joke that failed to amuse her. There was an upchinned tilt to her face now; a swift-rising resentment narrowed her eyes, squeezing the warmth from them. 'A man in town made me the same offer,' she reported. 'He said his name was Lee Monroe, and he seemed to think I'd jump at the chance.' Then she asked, 'Do I appear that cheap, Mr. Troop?'

Yet even now, and this was a thing that hugely impressed him, her voice retained its low-pitched tone. And although some inward heat of anger or embarrassment stained her

15

high-boned cheeks, she lost none of her queenly composure. Comparing her with other women he'd known, Lew Troop contemplated her with growing admiration. She was keen enough to guess what might be in a man's mind and possessed the courage to call the turn as she saw it. The thought came to him now that she must have been propositioned on countless occasions by men who felt as he did; by men whose heads were filled with fancy notions at the sight of her.

'I didn't mean it that way,' Troop said, endeavoring to make it sound right and doubting if he succeeded. He had never been much good at lying, even to a woman.

Fern Borgstrom didn't say anything for a long moment. She just looked at him, sizing him up in the way of a suspicious wife whose husband had stayed out all night. So Troop said, 'No strings attached. Just a favor for a lady.'

And because he meant it, what he said sounded right to him. It even made him feel good. He grinned at her and said, 'I mean that, ma'am—just a friendly favor.'

'So?' she murmured, her eyes steadily appraising. 'Well, I cannot accept a favor. But I'll give you a job, if you're looking for one.'

The sheer unexpectedness of it confused Lew Troop. What in God's name would a

16

Free Strip homesteader want with a hired man?

'A job?' he asked. 'Doing what?'

That seemed to surprise her. She peered at him as if thinking he must be dim-witted. 'Is it so strange that a woman should employ a hired man?'

'But what would he do?'

'Chores, of course. All kinds of chores. He would repair fences, corrals—anything that needs fixing. And there's a winter's supply of firewood to be hauled.'

Troop considered that explanation in silence for a moment before saying, 'A man's saddle wouldn't be much use to him, working a job like that. Or his rope.'

'There might be some calves to brand,' she suggested. 'My father owned a few cows, including a valuable Jersey heifer that I'll want brought in and penned. Does that make the job more appealing?'

Troop shook his head. A riding man would have to be tolerable hard up to take such a job. Even if he was flat broke and had a hunger grind in his guts, he'd think twice before turning hired man to a homesteader.

'Then you're not looking for a job?' she asked.

'Not in this country,' Troop explained. 'I'm partial to the desert for winter riding. Never

17

could abide cold weather. Snow wouldn't agree with me at all.'

'Is it the snow, or Dade Chastain?'

That bald-faced questioning of his courage angered Lew Troop. He looked her in the eye and said rankly, 'I said it was snow, didn't I? Well, that's what I mean—snow!'

She smiled, and as if thinking aloud, she murmured, 'I suppose Mr. Chastain might make it unpleasant for a homesteader's hired man.'

'You'll never have the chance to find out,' Troop predicted. And now he thought, her being a woman won't make any difference to Dade Chastain. A man would be a fool to get mixed up in such a deal, unless there was more than wages in it. He wondered if there might be, later on. He doubted it, and looking at her now, he was convinced that Fern Borgstrom would settle for nothing less than marriage. In which case there'd be no wages . . .

'It will be downright lonely out there on the Strip, all by yourself,' he warned. 'No near neighbors at all.'

She shrugged. Her attention shifted to the far hills, and for a moment she seemed lost in sober reflection. Then she said, 'There'll be neighbors after a while. A year from now there'll be a dozen families living on the Free

Strip, each one a monument to the memory of my father.'

'I doubt it,' Troop said. 'Your being a woman won't help you none with Dade Chastain. He'll run you off, regardless.'

She shook her head, refusing that prediction. 'Mr. Eggleston tried to talk me out of coming here, but he was very nice about it, and quite gentlemanly. He's the sheriff.'

Troop laughed. He said, 'Big Bill Eggleston is a ladies' man, but he's Chastain's man first, last, and all the time. You'll get no protection from him. Not a particle. This is cow country, ma'am, and Dade Chastain controls it.'

Fern Borgstrom shook her head again. 'Mr. Chastain will not control my land,' she said, and drove on.

CHAPTER THREE

Lew Troop crossed the ford, not looking back until he had rimmed the ridge east of Canteen Creek. Here he halted, rolling a cigarette and watching the distant wagon go along the west slope. Fern Borgstrom made a small shape on the high spring seat; against the vast backdrop of the Sun Dance Hills she looked helpless and forlorn, like a discarded doll perched on a

19

toy wagon. Watching her, Troop knew a moment of inexpressible sadness. It was like the feeling a man got sometimes while he crouched beside a lonely campfire at night; as if he had lost the trail and wouldn't ever find it again; an aching, gone-yonderly feeling.

Troop turned the grulla toward town. Why should the sight of a woman on a wagon affect him like this?

What happened to her was no skin off his rump. A saddle-bred man had no call to feel sorry for sodbusting homesteaders. They had strung their damned barbed wire across too much graze already. 'To hell with her,' he muttered.

He was within three miles of Signal when he met Sheriff Eggleston.

'So you finally got a hankerin' for town life,' the jowly-faced lawman said. 'How's things at the horse camp?'

'Fine,' Troop said. 'Just fine. Is Matt Shayne still serving cold beer at the Shamrock?'

'Colder'n a banker's heart,' Eggleston reported. 'Say, speakin' of beer, I'll buy you a dozen bottles if you'll take a message back to Chastain for me.'

'Not going back,' Troop said. 'Drawed my wages.'

Eggleston sighed and said enviously, 'You

young bucks sure got it nice. You pull your picket pin any time the notion strikes you, free as a ridge-runnin' stud. Wish I was like that. If it ain't cow thieves, it's fool nesters messin' things up. Did you meet a woman in a wagon back yonder?'

'Met several,' Troop said. 'Which one you mean?'

Eggleston showed his appreciation of the joke by loosing a burst of hearty laughter. 'That's rich,' he chortled, shaking his head. 'Probably ain't been another woman drove down this road in a month.' Then he said, 'I mean the double-breasted one with light chestnut hair and blue eyes. By God, she's a looker. I got to admit that. But she ain't got good sense. Wouldn't pay me no mind when I told her she was wastin' her time comin' out here. So now I got to ride fifteen miles to tell Chastain he has a new neighbor that needs vacatin'. Ain't that hell?'

'Yeah,' Troop agreed, and he had the queer feeling that he had never really seen Big Bill Eggleston before. Until this moment it hadn't occurred to him that there was anything wrong about Big Bill being a one-way lawman who consistently favored Slash C and closed his eyes to every raw deal Chastain put over on Free Strip settlers. But now, looking into Eggleston's flabby good-natured face, Troop

21

understood that Big Bill was a counterfeit sheriff who habitually neglected the duty he'd sworn to perform—the duty of protecting life and property against unlawful acts. Everyone in Cathedral Basin took Eggleston's one-way enforcement for granted, accepting his allegiance to Slash C as a matter of course.

Hell, I took it for granted myself, Troop thought. But it wasn't right, and the unfairness of it prompted him to say, 'Seems like you could give Swede's daughter a chance to move into her house before you sic Chastain onto her, Bill.'

'That'd only make it worse on everybody,' Eggleston said. 'Once they git settled down it's hard to budge 'em, short of shootin', and I don't want that. Shootin' scrapes git into the newspapers and make it look like a sheriff ain't on the job. We learnt our lesson with Swede Borgstrom. Dade wants to put the hustle on 'em smack-dab, before they git a toe hold. He'll have Swede's daughter off that place by noon tomorrow.'

'Hell of a way to treat a woman,' Troop muttered.

Eggleston nodded agreement. 'I tried to reason with her, so's all this wouldn't have to happen. But she has Swede's mule-stubborn ways. We can't have nesters spoilin' good cow country, Lew. You know that. Look what

22

they done over in Oxbow Valley. That was some of the best graze in Arizona until they plowed it up, tryin' to grow grain on it. Two dry years and the homesteaders went broke. had to pack up and git. But they'd ruint the land, for cattle or anythin' else.'

'One woman wouldn't do much plowing,' Troop suggested.

Eggleston snorted. 'You talk like a drunk sheepherder. If we let one sodbuster stay, we'd have a dozen more in six months' time. Especially a good-lookin' female like her. Hell, she'd attract more men than Belle Smith used to toll into the Bon Ton.'

'Used to? Don't she dance there any more?'

Big Bill shook his head. 'Ain't you heard?'

'Heard what?'

'About me buyin' the Palacial Hotel and hirin' Belle to run it for me. She was too good for that dance-hall grind. If she wasn't already married I might even think about hitchin' up with her, legal.'

'Didn't know she was a married woman,' Troop said. 'Never saw a wedding ring on her finger.'

Eggleston laughed. 'Belle quit her no-account husband six months ago and took back her maiden name. She's got ambition, that gal—knows how to git ahead in the world. You should see how she's improved

23

things at the Palacial. New carpet in the lobby, a pot in every commode, and hemp fire ropes in all the second-story rooms.'

'You planning to give Mayme Driscoll's parlor house some competition?' Troop asked slyly.

'Naw, nothin' like that, Lew. The Palacial is a first-class hotel—the best this side of Tucson. Well, guess I better hit a shuck toward Slash C.'

'Give my regards to God,' Troop suggested.

'God?'

'Dade Chastain,' Troop explained. 'He's God in Cathedral Basin.'

Eggleston laughed. 'Damned if he ain't, just about. You'd never think Dade rode into this country with just a rope and a runnin' iron twenty years ago. Well, have a good time in town, Lew. But no rough stuff.'

'No rough stuff,' Troop agreed, and rode on.

Contemplating what Eggleston had said about homesteaders, he supposed Big Bill was right, in a way. Sodbusters and cattlemen couldn't get along together in the same country. It had been that way in Texas and it was the same here. Cowmen wanted open range and the farmers built fences. One wanted the land left the way God made it and the other plowed it up. Troop had never bothered to see the homesteader's side of it. Being cowranch raised, he had a riding man's contempt for plow jockeys. A queer lot, he'd thought; a shiftless timid breed infringing upon the rights of better men. But he didn't feel that way about Fern Borgstrom.

He thought, She has more spunk than most men. Remembering how she'd said, 'It's my place and I shall live there,' he felt sorry for her. Being run off her place would be a bitter pill to swallow for so proud a woman. Swede's dream had turned into a nightmare for him and it would be worse than that for Fern Borgstrom. It would be like spoiling something nice and bright-shining. He wondered how her eyes would look when it was over; if they'd still have that unwavering self-confidence and the pride in them.

But presently, as the familiar sprawl of Signal's weather-beaten buildings loomed before him, Lew Troop's thinking turned to more pleasant things.

'Five weeks' thirst to quench,' he mused smilingly.

He wondered if Belle Smith would still treat him like kinfolk from Texas, now that she was the manager of a first-class hotel; and how it would feel to dance with the big blonde at the Bon Ton . . .

Signal hadn't changed at all. The same

limp-bodied loafers occupied the same benches on the shaded side of Ledbetter's Livery; the Shamrock Saloon beer was as cold as Troop remembered it, and the barbershop bath as hot. By sundown he was sheared and shaved, had renewed a few acquaintances, and had eaten a bounteous supper at the Chink's Café. The cigar he smoked was mild, the bourbon he drank was mellow. But within one hour's time Lew Troop realized there was something wrong with his celebration. It didn't give him the familiar lift. It hadn't produced the fine sense of well-being that a man should feel on his first night in town. He visited the Palacial lobby, hoping to meet Belle Smith, but she was nowhere around so he quartered across Main Street toward the Shamrock again.

Doc Pendergast, a portly pill-pusher with a weakness for bourbon whisky, was the saloon's only bar customer. He stood with his bulging midriff cradled against the counter's beveled edge and voiced his opinion of the Lincoln County War, which had recently ended.

'The Murphy–Chisum feud bears out my philosophy,' he orated to Matt Shayne. 'Man's hope of attaining perpetual peace is a witless dream.'

Troop drank a beer, observing that the

usual low-limit stud game was in progress at the rear table with Ike Ledbetter, Joe Shedrow, Lee Monroe, and a Tucson whisky drummer as players. When Matt Shayne finished serving him, Doc Pendergast started up again, directing his free-flowing talk at the patient barkeep.

'There will never be real peace,' Pendergast insisted. 'All you have to do is get three people together in one room, or one house, or one county, and you'll have friction. That is fundamental. It's not a case of attempting to side-step trouble, or of running away from it, or turning the other cheek. The urge for conflict is an essential ingredient of the human race. It is part of what we call human nature— a nature conceived in passion and born in pain; a prepotent, changeless nature spawned in the Garden of Eden and renewed in the fertile wombs of women generation after generation!'

Matt Shayne nodded his bald head in solemn agreement. 'That's right, bejasus. 'Tis the wimmin that are the root of it.'

Troop grinned, knowing that Shayne was bossed by a reedy little wife half his size. He sauntered over to the poker table and accepted Ledbetter's invitation to sit in. 'For about half an hour is all,' he announced.

He won the first three pots.

Lee Monroe, who drove a jerk-line freight outfit for Ledbetter, called for a new deck. He was younger than his brother Monk and much less beefy, but he had the same overbearing brutish way about him. Remembering what Fern Borgstrom had reported, Troop took a secret satisfaction in besting the mule-skinner at cards.

Joe Shedrow, a meek and shabby man, won the fourth hand, raking in a small pot with obvious thankfulness. Then, on the fifth deal, Troop tangled with Monroe in a betting duel that drove the others out.

'You act like you might have aces,' Monroe muttered, studying the four exposed cards in front of Troop. 'But I'm bettin' you ain't.'

He boosted the bet an additional dollar.

Troop knew he had the mule-skinner beaten; knew he had a mortal cinch. The best Monroe could have was a pair of aces, queen high. But Troop didn't sound overly confident when he said, 'Up one,' and pushed out two silver dollars.

'Whew!' Joe Shedrow exclaimed. 'What a pot!'

'Must be better'n ten dollars in it,' the whisky drummer observed.

Monroe called the bet, and then cursed as Troop turned over his hole card—an ace, giving him a pair of aces king high against

28

Monroe's aces, queen high. 'Of all the goddamn stinkin' Irish luck!'

Troop raked in the pot. He pocketed his winnings and pushed back his chair. 'So you think the Irish stink.'

'Supposin' I do?' Monroe demanded irritably.

'My mother was Irish,' Troop said flatly, and motioned for him to get up.

'What you tryin' to do, start a fight?' Monroe demanded. He glanced at Troop's holstered Colt, adding, 'I got no gun.'

'Well, you've got fists—which is all you'll need.'

Over at the bar Doc Pendergast continued to spout his profound opinions, declaring, 'Man is bred for conflict. His first experience upon being born is to be slapped on the behind.'

Lee Monroe eased back in his chair. But he didn't get up. He shifted his tobacco quid from one cheek to the other. He forced a chuckle and said blandly, 'I got nothin' agin the Irish. Not a thing. Sit down and we'll play some more poker.'

Yellow, Troop thought, and was surprised that a brother of Monk Monroe should be afraid to fight. He said, 'I've had enough,' and walked to the doorway. He felt let down. Even though he was twenty-some dollars winner, he

29

felt cheated.

When Troop entered the Bon Ton Dance Hall a well-padded blonde girl came quickly up to him, saying, 'I heard you was in town. What made you stay away so long, handsome?'

'Earning money to spend on you,' Troop said, and led her to one of the tables that bordered the dance floor. He ordered two drinks and asked, 'How you been doing, Grace?'

'Just fine, Lew. I been doing real good since Belle Smith quit.'

She sat bent forward with both elbows on the table, her low-cut blouse revealing the cleavage of ample breasts. Five weeks ago Lew Troop had thought her pretty. . .

'Why so gloomy?' Grace asked, reaching over to pat his hand.

Troop shrugged. 'Stayed at the horse camp too long,' he muttered. 'Must've caught cabin fever.'

A waiter came up to the table and said to Grace, 'There's a gent at the door asking to see you.'

She peered toward the doorway. 'Tell him to come back later,' she said, and as the waiter departed, she added smilingly, 'That Lee Monroe thinks he's the only good-looking man in town. He's a spender, though—a real

30

sport, especially with a few drinks under his belt.'

'Shouldn't wonder,' Troop said, not much interested.

What, he wondered, was the matter with him? Nothing he'd done tonight seemed worth the doing.

'Perhaps a dance would cheer you up,' Grace suggested.

It should have, for she arched her body against him so that the dance was a lingering and intimate embrace. But even then, with her blonde head tilted back and her eyes so frankly inviting, Troop couldn't discard the mood that had cloaked him all evening. When the dance was over he left, using a pretext that he had to meet a man at the Shamrock on business. But he didn't go to the saloon; he went into the Palacial lobby and said to the clerk, 'I want to see the manager.'

'She's busy right now,' the pimply-faced youth announced.

'So am I,' Troop said, and grabbed him by the shirt front. 'What room is she in?'

'F-f-first d-d-door to the left at the top of the s-s-stairs,' the clerk stuttered. 'N-number One.'

'You're learning,' Troop said, and turned up the stairway.

He had to knock twice before there was an

answer. 'Who is it?' came Belle Smith's voice.

'Your country cousin from Texas,' Troop announced.

A key turned in the lock, the door opened, and Belle exclaimed, 'Lew! Wherever have you been all these weeks?'

She looked as if she'd just got out of a bathtub. She wore a red silk kimono and her dark curls were tied with a red ribbon on top of her head. She said smilingly, 'Come on in, Lew, and make yourself at home.' She scurried ahead of him to clear the room's only chair of lacy underthings.

Troop tossed his hat onto the bed. He sat down and thought, This is more like it! He watched her go to the bureau and pour two drinks from a fancy square-shaped bottle. When she handed him a thimble-sized glass he sniffed the drink and asked, 'What is it?'

'Benedictine,' Belle said. 'It's good for your gizzard.'

'Do I rub it on, or drink it?'

'Neither one, foolish. You sip it.'

Troop sipped, and made a face. 'I'll still take bourbon.'

Then he asked, 'What's this I hear about Big Bill Eggleston beating my time with you?'

Belle laughed. 'Who you funnin'? Bill Eggleston is forty-five and 'way too old for me. Why, I'm scarcely past my twenty-first birthday.'

Liar, Troop thought, guessing she was closer to thirty.

'This is just a business deal,' Belle explained. 'I got tired of being pawed by dance-hall sports for two bits a feel. Of course, Big Bill thinks he's quite a ladies' man himself, but I've been able to handle him fine, so far.'

She put the glasses away and then sat on his lap. 'How long you going to be in town, Lew?'

'Not long,' Troop said. He decided she had put on a few pounds. 'I quit at Slash C. I'll be heading south directly.'

'You're fiddle-footed,' Belle censured. She ran her fingers through his black hair, deliberately mussing it. 'But you're nice. I'd like to take a trip myself—a little vacation. Why don't we take a stage ride to Tucson? You could go on from there, Lew.'

'Wouldn't want to leave my horse,' Troop said, sorry now that he had come up here. 'You don't come by a pony like Blue every day.'

'Or a girl like me,' Belle suggested.

Troop grinned. 'That's right,' he agreed. There was nothing wrong with Belle. But there was something wrong with him. . .

'You could come back with me on the stage and get your horse,' Belle suggested. 'We'd have a lot of fun.'

Troop shook his head. 'Cost too much.'

'I'll pay the fares for both of us,' Belle offered eagerly. 'I've got quite a bit saved up, Lew. Enough so we can have a high old time in Tucson.'

'You'll never have enough to pay my fare anywhere.'

Belle laughed. 'You and your Texas pride.' She ran her fingers through his hair again. Then she whispered, 'You ain't kissed me yet, honey.'

He did, then; but it didn't mean anything to him. Not a thing. Troop couldn't understand it. And neither could Belle. She leaned back, pouting at him. 'You sick or something?'

Troop shrugged. He had thought she was prettier than a red-wheeled wagon. He looked into her heart-shaped face, wondering why she didn't seem so to him now; why the clinging pressure of her lips hadn't stirred him at all. She hadn't changed, that he could see. Her eyes still danced, her lips were as red as they had always been, her black hair was as curly and sweet-scented . . .

'I guess,' Troop said, 'I'd better be going.'

Belle stared at him in disbelief. 'But you just got here!' she exclaimed, not moving until he started to get up from the chair. Then she got off his lap and complained, 'I don't see

34

you for a month, and then you just say hello and good-by. That's no way to treat a girl, Lew. You act like you don't even like me.'

'Sure I like you, Belle,' Troop said, but his voice was impatient and he picked up his hat.

When he opened the door Belle demanded, 'What did you come up here for, anyway?'

Troop turned and looked at her and knew she had a case on him; more of a case than he'd ever imagined. He hadn't thought she was the kind that would go romantic over a man. Not really. But the wet-eyed look of her now convinced him. He wished there was some way he could explain how he felt tonight. But how could he, when he didn't understand it himself?

He said, 'I'll see you again, Belle,' and was softly cursing as he went down the stairs. This celebration had gone as flat as stale beer.

Sheriff Eggleston came into the lobby, slapping trail dust from his shoulders. He said disgustedly, 'Four hours' saddle-polishing my pants on account of a fool woman. She shouldn't of gone out there in the first place.'

'Did God send his angels to warn Miss Borgstrom?' Troop asked.

'Done it hisself,' Eggleston said. He frowned and rubbed his nose and added, 'I sort of felt sorry for her. She looked like she'd been cryin'—like Swede's ghost was hauntin' her.'

Troop glanced at the well-polished star pinned to Eggleston's vest. He reached out and touched it and said, 'Looks like silver. Feels like silver.'

'What did you think it was?' Big Bill asked.

'Tin,' Troop said, and continued on across the lobby.

'Just what in hell you mean by that?' Eggleston called after him. When Troop went outside without answering, Big Bill peered at the pimply-faced clerk and asked, 'What did he mean?'

'I think he's daft,' the clerk said politely. 'I really do, Mr. Eggleston.'

'*Sheriff* Eggleston!' Big Bill corrected angrily. 'Don't anybody know I'm sheriff around here?'

CHAPTER FOUR

Lew Troop was standing at the Shamrock bar, half drunk and paying no attention to the other customers, when he heard the name Borgstrom. Turning around, he saw Lee Monroe talking to Dade Chastain.

'It was sure comical,' Monroe related. 'There was Big Bill talkin' to her like an uncle, sayin' how foolish it would be for her to take over Swede's place, and all the time he wagged his jaw she was buyin' enough provisions to last her for six months. I guess she figgers you wouldn't run off a pretty woman.'

Dade Chastain showed no amusement. 'Her being pretty makes no difference at all,' he said in his sharp, precise voice. 'Not a particle of difference. I told her to move, with Sheriff Bill for a witness that she got proper notice.'

'How much time did you give her?' Monroe inquired.

'She's to be off the place by noon tomorrow,' Chastain said.

He was, Troop thought, a thoroughly ruthless and thoroughly efficient man. Unlike most owners of big outfits, Chastain didn't employ a foreman. He was his own ramrod, and a hard-driving one. The Slash C crew had no real liking for their boss, but his unwavering arrogance commanded their respect.

Now Chastain said, 'Her being pretty won't furnish winter feed for a single Slash C cow. That's what I'm interested in—cows.'

Lee Monroe laughed, maneuvering his tobacco chaw so that it bulged his right cheek. 'I'm more partial to wimmin myself at this time of year with winter comin' on. Never knowed a cow that'd keep a man warm on a cold night.'

Lew Troop stood there, not drunk but not entirely sober. This talk about a sorrel-haired woman shouldn't concern him, he thought. She was nothing to him. Not a goddamn thing. Just someone he'd met on the road and passed the time of day with. In fact, she'd been uppity, and a trifle sharp with her tongue, asking if it was snowballs or Chastain he was afraid of. Even though it didn't seem quite fitting for Fern Borgstrom to be a topic for saloon gossip, it was none of his affair.

'When you run her off I hope she moves into town,' Monroe was saying, loud enough for all to hear. He gave Chastain a wise smile, adding, 'She's got a look in them eyes of her'n, like she'd be real good company on a cold night.'

He was still smiling when Lew Troop stepped up and hit him in the face.

Monroe fell back along the bar, tripped over a cuspidor, and went down. 'What the hell!' he blurted, gawking up at Troop.

Dade Chastain seemed equally astonished. He peered at Troop, demanding, 'Why'd you hit him?'

Troop didn't understand it himself. He hadn't planned it. A flare of fierce resentment had propelled him; an urge so elemental that he had acted upon pure impulse. He thought fleetingly, I must be drunk, and knew he wasn't. Not that drunk.

Lee Monroe got up, gingerly fingering the bridge of his bleeding nose. 'You gone loco?' he demanded.

'Don't talk about a lady that way,' Troop said, and observing the pallor of Monroe's cheeks, he wondered at it. The man looked sick.

'Lady?' Monroe asked. 'You call her a lady?'

Troop nodded. 'If you think otherwise, put up your fists.'

Matt Shayne leaned over the bar, wagging a rub rag at Troop. 'Now, we'll have no more shenanigans in here, bejasus! If it's fightin' you want, go outside!'

And Doc Pendergast, still propped against the bar, proclaimed loudly, 'That proves my point, Matt. The human race was bred for conflict!'

Neither Shayne nor anyone else paid Pendergast the slightest attention. They were all looking at Lew Troop. Monroe stared at him in bug-eyed disbelief. 'Since when did Slash C riders start stickin' up for homesteader wimmin?' he asked, thoroughly puzzled. Then he turned to Chastain, demanding, 'How about it, Dade?'

Chastain shrugged. 'He quit today.'

But that didn't solve the puzzle for Lee Monroe. He said, 'You must be drunk.'

Then, as he held a bandanna to his bleeding nose and gagged, Troop noticed that Monroe's cheek was no longer bulged by a tobacco quid. Lee had swallowed his chew. He retched and hurried toward the doorway, the bandanna clamped over his mouth and his other hand holding his stomach. At the batwing gates he turned and tried to say something, and couldn't. Then he went out to the sidewalk.

For a long moment Monroe's strangled heaving was the only sound in the room.

Stark sober now, Troop understood that he was the target of attention. Matt Shayne stood behind the bar methodically wiping a glass over and over. Five card players, attracted by the scuffle, stood in a half circle as if expecting additional entertainment. Only Doc Pendergast seemed oblivious of the tension that was like a tight-strung wire.

'You shouldn't of hit Lee like that,' Shayne said censuringly. 'Lee wasn't even talkin' to you.'

'Just human nature asserting its essential stress,' Doc Pendergast insisted cheerfully, and now, as Lee Monroe called to him from the batwings, the old medico reluctantly departed.

Troop was increasingly aware of Dade Chastain's narrow-eyed appraisal. The dour-faced cowman peered at him in the questing fashion of a cattle buyer calculating the weight of a prime steer.

'What you gawking at?' Troop asked.

'At a drunk, or a damned fool,' Chastain muttered. 'I'm not sure which.' Then he asked, 'You heading south tomorrow, like you planned?'

Until this moment there had been no doubt on that score in Lew Troop's mind. But now, sensing what lay behind Chastain's question and resenting it, he asked, 'Make any difference to you where I ride?'

'None at all, just so you stay away from the Free Strip.'

That seemed to amuse Joe Shedrow, who loosed a cackling chuckle.

Chastain frowned at the wood peddler. He demanded, 'What's so comical?'

'Nothin',' Shedrow said, the smile fading from his thin cheeks. 'Nothin' at all, Mr. Chastain.'

But Lew Troop understood why Shedrow had chuckled. Joe was remembering how that same ultimatum had been given him; how he'd been told he could settle anywhere he chose, except on the only land available for homesteading. There were others like him in

Signal; shabby, disillusioned men who'd tried to establish homes. Furtive, petty-thieving men turned into shiftless failures by Dade Chastain's domination of Free Strip grass.

The Slash C owner turned back to Troop and said, 'You better ride south tomorrow, just like you planned.'

'That wouldn't be a warning, would it?'

'Call it anything you choose, but be gone from here tomorrow.'

The monstrous arrogance of that command was like a slap in the face; like a casual, backhanded slap. It was as if Chastain considered him no better than a spineless plow jockey—some white-trash nester told to skedaddle. Yet even so, smarting from the bald insult of it, Troop tried to tell himself that he should do as Chastain suggested. A man would be a fool to let a little pride upset his plans. It wasn't as if he *wanted* to remain in Cathedral Basin. Far from it. This was no country to spend a winter in. The snow, he'd heard, drifted six feet deep during blizzards, and God only knew how cold it got. But the arrogance he saw in Chastain's eyes ruined that fine reasoning.

'Maybe I won't leave tomorrow,' Troop said. 'Maybe I'll wait around and see how a big outfit runs a woman off her homestead.'

There was no change in Dade Chastain's

high-beaked frowning face. But a metallic shine came to his eyes, and Troop thought instantly, I've got a fight on my hands!

The conviction that this was so—that Dade Chastain wouldn't back down in front of an audience—scratched along Troop's nerves like barbed brush. By God, he'd done it now! He'd got himself snagged in his own damn rope!

And for what?

For no reason, Troop reflected disgustedly. No reason at all. Except pride. And what the hell good was pride? Just a worthless trinket worn by witless fools who talked too much. In this black moment of self-condemnation Troop remembered bunkhouse gossip he'd heard about Dade Chastain's ability with a gun. He wondered how much of it was true. . .

Chastain eased away from the bar so that his right arm hung free. He said, 'So you're asking for a fight. Is that it, bronc-stomper?'

Matt Shayne, who'd continued wiping the same glass all this time, now blurted, 'Not in here, Dade! No shootin' in here!'

'Shut up,' Chastain snapped, not turning his head.

Shayne sighed, accepting the rebuke without question, and hurried along the bar, toting glass and rub rag with him.

43

The Big Mogul, Troop thought. So goddamn big he could order men around in their own establishments. Chastain's assertion that he ran the whole of Cathedral Basin had seemed amusing, out there in the Slash C yard. But it didn't seem so now.

'Well,' Chastain asked, 'you want to try your luck—or leave town like you planned?'

It was, Troop understood, a chance to avoid a shootout. 'Like you planned,' he guessed, was Dade's way of making it easy for him to skedaddle. Chastain knew how to pressure a man. He was an expert at forcing men to tuck their tails between their legs. Dade knew how to shape a showdown, and he was wanting one now. No doubt about it.

Troop thought, I'm a fool for getting into this. But he couldn't slough off his Texas pride. He said, 'I'll give my luck a try.'

He thought Chastain would make his draw right then, and was muscle-cocked with expectancy. Matching that draw wouldn't be enough. A man had to beat it to survive.

But Chastain said, 'Your luck might not be so good.'

Troop shrugged, his angular face revealing none of the tension in him. There was a picture on the wall behind Chastain—a voluptuous reclining nude whose nakedness was accentuated by a dark divan, and whose

44

face, directly above Chastain's right shoulder, reminded Troop of Fern Borgstrom. It had the same half-smiling expression.

Damn her, he thought. And now, with startling clarity, Troop knew what had spoiled his night in town; he understood why neither blonde Grace nor black-haired Belle Smith had been able to lighten his mood. Fern Borgstrom had turned him loco in the head!

'You still feel lucky?' Chastain asked.

Perspiration dribbled from Troop's armpits. Dade, he supposed, was playing this according to an established custom used against unwelcome nesters. Chastain knew how suspense could rub a man's nerves raw; how waiting could rattle a man and throw him off balance. 'Sweating a chump,' the border bunch called it.

Chastain moved a step to the left, as if not liking the angle of chandelier lamplight. Shayne was at one end of the bar now, the five poker players at the other. A ranch wagon rolled along Main Street, that slight commotion sounding loud against the saloon's strict silence.

'Try your luck, if you think it's good,' Chastain suggested.

There was a higher pitch to his voice, and Troop wondered about it. Anger did that to some men, lifting their tone to tenor key when the blood lust was in them; when the itch to kill became a thrusting, overwhelming need. Or it could mean something else . . .

Was Chastain bluffing? Was that why he hadn't drawn his gun?

It occurred to Troop that Dade had no way of knowing what he was up against in gun skill. Dade wasn't accustomed to having his commands disobeyed. Men didn't accept his challenge; they did what he told them, or left Cathedral Basin. They took his warnings and high-tailed for the tules.

Was that why he didn't grab?

Troop smiled thinly, thinking, If he was bluffing, he got called.

Then the batwing gates creaked and Big Bill Eggleston came across the room demanding, 'Lew, what's the idea of knockin' Lee Monroe down?'

Eggleston's voice wasn't overly loud. But in this hushed room it was like shouting.

'I didn't,' Troop said, not shifting his gaze from Chastain until Eggleston moved in between them. 'Monroe tripped over a spittoon and fell down.'

'But you hit him,' the sheriff insisted. 'You busted his nose. He's over to Doc Pendergast's house now, havin' it splinted.'

'So?' Troop mused, surprised that he had hit Monroe that hard.

46

'He wants you locked up for assault and battery,' Eggleston said. 'Why'd you hit him?'

Troop shrugged. Big Bill turned to Chastain. 'You see the fight, Dade?'

'It wasn't a fight,' Chastain muttered, and eased back against the bar. 'It was malicious assault, pure and simple. Lee was talking to me about Swede Borgstrom's daughter. He didn't look at Troop or speak to him. But Troop stepped up and slugged Lee and told him to quit talking about her.'

Eggleston turned to Troop, his eyes wide with bafflement. 'You're cow folks, Lew. You ain't no nester lover.' Then he went thoughtful, rubbing his bulbous nose. 'Leastwise, you wasn't before you met Swede's daughter.'

'I don't like to hear a decent woman run down,' Troop muttered.

Eggleston kept rubbing his nose. He said suspiciously, 'You must of done more than tip your hat to that dame when you met her on the stage road. You ain't figgerin' to see her agin, are you?'

'What if I am?' Troop demanded. 'What goddamn business is it of yours?'

'Now, take it easy,' Big Bill cautioned. 'Don't git your hackles up with me.'

'Then quit prying into my private affairs,' Troop said.

47

As if thinking aloud, Eggleston said softly, 'Swede's daughter remarked to me that she would need a hired man.' He rubbed his nose again and gave Troop a squint-eyed look and asked, 'You wouldn't be plannin' to work for her, would you, Lew?'

'Does that concern you, one way or the other?' Troop demanded, his voice rank with resentment. And then, with futile, frustrating anger prodding him, Troop announced, 'Sure I am. I start working for her tomorrow morning.'

He glanced at Chastain, observing the brief astonishment in that man's milk-blue eyes and hugely enjoying it. Who the hell did these two bastards think they were, telling him what he couldn't do?

'A cowboy workin' for a nester?' Sheriff Eggleston demanded. 'Doin' what?'

'Depends on what needs doing,' Troop said. He looked at Chastain with a go-to-hell grin slanting his cheeks, and turned toward the doorway.

For a full moment, while he walked to the batwings and went through them, there was an odd shocked silence in the saloon. Then Dade Chastain predicted sourly, 'He'll be out of a job at noon tomorrow.'

Ignoring that prediction, Troop angled across Main Street's moonlit dust, feeling

48

queerly spent. He stopped in front of the hotel and shaped up a cigarette and then stood there with it forgotten in his fingers. What a fool he'd been! What a jug-headed, prideful fool!

It was bad enough getting into a showdown squabble with Chastain, who might have been fast enough to outdraw him. Luck, or Dade's caution, had got him out of that. But instead of letting well enough alone, he'd gone and talked himself into hiring out as handy man to a homesteader.

Troop hadn't thought he was drunk. But now, standing here with a chill breeze fanning his face, he decided he must have been drunk. Nobody but a booze-addled chump would have done what he did. Matt Shayne should put him on the Injun list. A bartender shouldn't sell whisky to a half-wit.

Troop cursed, and stuck the cigarette between his frown-twisted lips. He thumbed a match aflame and took a deep drag of smoke. He'd been potted, all right. No doubt of it. Shayne must be mixing his bourbon with bootleg rotgut. He'd thought it seemed a trifle rank, after the first few drinks. It reminded him of the pulque that peons drank across the border.

Joe Shedrow came across the street, walking in the furtive back-glancing way of a spooky man. He stepped up to the plank
49

walk, glanced at the saloon, and said gustily, 'You told Chastain off, by grab! You told him good!'

'So what?' Troop muttered, wanting no cheap-John praise from the likes of Shedrow.

'You done somethin' I didn't have the brass to do when Chastain barred me off the Strip. You stood up to him, by grab. It was purely elegant to see.'

Troop flipped his cigarette away. He said, 'Maybe Chastain's bark is worse'n his bite. I've met that kind before.'

'I wish Sheriff Eggleston hadn't come in like he did,' Joe said. 'I wish you'd of gunned Chastain down. If ever a man deserved killin', he does.'

'You talk,' Troop suggested, 'like a man with a God-awful grudge.'

'I got reason to,' Shedrow muttered, his voice vibrant with emotion. 'Dade Chastain was the cause of me losin' the nicest wife a man ever had.'

Troop shrugged, taking no interest in this man's troubles. Shedrow wasn't the first nester who'd had a wife die on him, or the first to blame it on some cowman, never admitting that it might have been hard work and short rations that killed her. The way some homesteaders worked their womenfolk was a caution.

'Reckon I'd better leave town before Big Bill takes a notion to arrest me,' Troop said, and turned away.

But Shedrow said urgently, 'There's five or six others like me—fellers that've been pushed around by them Slash C toughs. We ain't much account at fightin' with guns, but if we had somebody like you to . . .'

'Hell, I'm no sodbuster,' Troop interrupted impatiently.

'But you hired out to Miss Borgstrom,' Shedrow argued. 'That means you'll be buckin' a big outfit and will need help.'

Troop laughed at him. 'Help—from homesteaders?'

Then he walked toward Ledbetter's Livery.

★   ★   ★

Lee Monroe came out of the Palacial lobby with a bandage on his nose and a holstered gun at his hip. He wondered if Sheriff Eggleston had arrested Lew Troop and hoped he hadn't. There was only one way to fix that bastard. With a bullet. And it made no difference how he got it—front or back.

Monroe cursed, recalling how Troop had bested him at every turn tonight. First the poker game, beating him pot after pot. Then Troop had corralled Grace ahead of him. And

51

finally that wholly unexpected punch in the nose. Monroe winced, just thinking about it. There was still a throbbing ache all across his temples.

Why had Troop had it in for him? What reason did the dirty son have for persecuting a man like that? He'd done nothing to Troop.

Now, as Monroe observed a man moving across the dark street, he drew his gun, thinking it might be Troop. But when the yonder shape was outlined against the saloon's front window he muttered, 'Shedrow,' and holstered his gun. Troop, he supposed, was still at the bar, giving Matt's customers a chance to gawk at him. Eggleston wouldn't relish the idea of tangling with a tough Texan. And that Troop was tough. Dirty, stinking, lowdown tough!

Monroe crossed the street and was passing Mitchell's Mercantile when a girl on the dance-hall stoop called, 'Is that you, Lee?'

Monroe grimaced. That was a woman for you—always wagging her jaw at the wrong time. He turned and motioned to her, not wanting his voice heard at the saloon.

But she called, 'I'm through work, handsome.'

Monroe cursed. Couldn't she see he was in no mood to be bothered by women? He went back to the Bon Ton stoop and said, 'Some other time, Grace. I'm busy now—like you was earlier this evenin'.'

'What's the bandage for?' She peered at his face and giggled and asked, 'Where'd you get that black eye?'

'I've got no time for chatter now,' Monroe muttered, and went on toward the Shamrock.

If Troop was in there he would give it to him cold turkey.

CHAPTER FIVE

The livery stable was dark as a stack of stove lids. Troop collided with a bucket as he felt his way along the rank-odored runway. Someone—Ike Ledbetter, he supposed—was asleep in the harness room, his gusty snoring uninterrupted as Troop led his horse out of the first stall.

Lighting a match, Troop located his gear and began saddling in the dark. It was close to midnight now, time for respectable folks to be in their blankets. Fern Borgstrom was probably in bed, but she wouldn't be sleeping. Not after what Dade Chastain had told her. He grinned, thinking how surprised she'd be when he showed up at her place tomorrow morning.

A draft of air, cold and sharp against the barn's pungent warmth, swept down the long runway, and Troop thought, Back door must've blown open. He buttoned up his brush jacket. It seemed as if the weather was turning colder; might be snowing up in the Sun Dance Hills right now. He wondered if Doc Pendergast had finished fixing Lee Monroe's nose, and chuckled, recalling how Lee had swallowed his chaw. The mule-skinner had looked sicker than seven colicky calves. Lee wouldn't be so handsome with a busted beak.

Troop had his spurs buckled and was on the point of leading Blue outside when he heard footsteps behind him. Whirling instantly, he drew his gun. He stepped around the grulla and probed the yonder darkness and wondered who would be using the stable's rear door at this time of night.

Was it Chastain, wanting to finish the deal Big Bill had interrupted? Or was it Lee Monroe?

Convinced that it must be one or the other, Troop stood listening with his gun cocked. He was like that, with all his senses keyed for instant firing, when a voice called softly, 'It's me—Joe Shedrow.'

Astonishment pushed the tension out of Troop. 'You trying to get yourself shot?' he demanded.

Shedrow came up, making an obscure shape in the darkness. 'Lee Monroe is gunnin' for you. He's out there betwixt the blacksmith shop and the feed store.'

Recalling how he had scorned this man's offer of help, Troop said, 'I'm obliged to you, Joe. Real obliged.'

'You'd better leave by the back door,' Shedrow suggested. 'You can go through the corral and—'

'Me? Run from a goddamn mule-skinner?'

'But he's got a gun,' Shedrow insisted.

'So have I,' Troop said, and eased through the wide front doorway.

Main Street seemed less dark after the stable's deep-clotted blackness. Even though the sky was overcast with few stars showing, it wasn't so dark out here. The dance hall had closed, but the Shamrock Saloon's lamps still fashioned yellow patterns across the sidewalk. One upstairs window of the hotel was lighted, Troop noticed. Belle Smith's corner room, he thought, and grimaced, remembering how it had been up there.

Troop peered at the blacksmith shop, which was set back a trifle beyond the sidewalk, forming a long bay between the feed store to the east and Mitchell's Mercantile on the west. Monroe, he supposed, was waiting

55

at the corner. Expecting him to be on horseback, Lee would be expecting hoof tromp and a high target that would be easy to hit. The sneaky son might get a surprise.

Keeping close to building fronts, Troop started along the sidewalk, wanting to reach a position directly across from the blacksmith shop. Luck played a big part in a nighttime fracas, but the advantage was with the man who attacked. Troop grinned, recalling how surprised Shedrow had been because he had chosen to face Monroe instead of running away from him. It seemed odd that Joe had lived for forty years without learning that a man couldn't outrun trouble. No matter how fast he ran, nor how far, it always caught up with him. The world was well populated with Lee Monroes. If you ducked away from one in Signal, there'd be another waiting for you in Prescott, or Tucson, or Tombstone. . .

The faint tinkle of his spur rowels brought Troop to an abrupt halt. He was almost opposite the blacksmith shop now, near enough so that Monroe might hear him. Troop cursed his carelessness in not thinking to remove his spurs back there in the barn. He went down on one knee, intending to take them off, and at this precise instant a bullet whanged above his bent back.

Still bent over, Troop fired at a brief beacon

of muzzle flare. Side-stepping hastily, he was startled by the explosion of another gun diagonally across the dark street.

Not just Monroe! he thought in astonishment, and faded back against the barred windows of the Wells Fargo office. Lee Monroe wasn't satisfied to set a one-gun ambush; the mule-skinner had himself an assistant. Troop glanced back at the livery, calculating the distance he would have to cover in order to reach the barn doorway. There was a time to attack and a time to retreat. A man would be a fool to march down this street against *two* hidden guns.

Then, as a blast came from the darkness between him and the stable, Troop understood that he was trapped—that there'd be no returning to Ledbetter's Livery. They were out to get him. Not just Lee Monroe, but Chastain and Eggleston!

Troop held his fire, knowing they would use the telltale bloom for a target. A cold breeze ran along the street, stirring up a smell of risen dust. Troop thought, They're not sure just where I am, and took hope in this supposition. That first bullet had been the one. So close he'd heard the whanging air lash of its passage. Lady Luck had her arm around him then.

A dog began barking on some back street

and a woman's shrill voice commanded, 'Come back here, Spot!'

The gun beyond the feed store blasted again, and again, its random slugs ripping into the plank sidewalk. That, Troop supposed, was Lee Monroe, trying for a lucky shot. Troop was tempted to send a bullet at the mule-skinner, to try for a lucky shot himself. But that would give all three of them a target, and three to one was too damned much. If there was someplace he could fort up— anyplace except this open sidewalk.

A man stuck his head out of an upstairs window at the Palacial and complained, 'Why don't you goddamn drunks go home!'

That reminded Troop of a passageway that ran back between the hotel and Wimple's Saddle Shop. If he could reach that narrow alley, he'd have a good chance to make a fight of this.

It wasn't far; not more than fifty feet or so. And his boots wouldn't make much noise in the street's deep dust. It seemed like his best chance. His only chance.

Troop fired a single shot at Monroe, wanting to focus attention here, and was running toward the alley as those three guns exploded in unison. There was a sound of shattered glass and the twang of a bullet bouncing off an iron bar. In this moment, with all that racket echoing along Main Street, Troop thought he was going to make it unobserved. But when the shooting ceased his jingling spur rowels were a giveaway.

'There he goes!' Lee Monroe shouted.

Those goddamn spurs!

A bullet slammed into the sidewalk as Troop crossed it. Another ripped splinters from the hotel veranda railing. Troop misjudged the opening and collided with a corner of the saddle shop. Then, lunging on into the alley's quilted darkness, he tripped on a packing crate and fell headlong, dropping his gun.

But even so, all spraddled out and momentarily disarmed, Lew Troop felt a rising exultation. He had made it across the street, by God! With three guns blasting as him, he'd got in here without a scratch!

Searching frantically for his gun, Troop heard Big Bill Eggleston shout, 'Head him off out back!'

A slug plunked into a board above him, showering his hat with splinters. He cursed, knowing that he had to get out of here before they got around behind the hotel. He clawed for his gun, and found it, and heard a man ask indignantly, 'What in God's name is going on out there?'

'We've got Lew Troop boxed in the alley!'

Sheriff Eggleston shouted. 'He's gone loco and shootin' up the town!'

So that's how they've framed it, Troop thought. They intended to make this look like a legal deal, as if a drunken drifter had gone berserk. There'd be no stink raised about such a killing; no suspicion that it was other than the necessary shooting of a booze-crazed renegade.

Troop swore softly, seeing the sure hand of Dade Chastain in this. Now, as voices sounded out back, he understood that the dropped gun had trapped him. He took a step deeper into the alley, then froze as something slapped against his hat and came slithering past his right shoulder. He struck out wildly, hitting nothing. And in this moment of utter confusion Troop heard a whispering voice above him urge, 'Come up the fire rope!'

Belle Smith's voice.

Troop stood there for an instant, too astonished for rational thinking. What the hell did she mean about coming up a fire rope? Then, as Belle urged, 'Hurry, Lew!' he understood what she meant. Holstering his gun, Troop grasped the dangling rope and went up it, hand over hand.

He was panting when he crawled through the window. Panting and chuckling. For a moment, while Belle hastily pulled up the fire rope, Troop lay on the floor getting his wind, thinking happily that it had taken the combined efforts of Lady Luck and Belle Smith to bring him here.

'I heard you stumble over something down there,' Belle said, crouching beside him. 'It sure is lucky that this room has a side window.'

'And that you were in it,' Troop said gustily. He reached out and patted her shoulder and loosed a long sigh. 'Never thought you'd be the one to save my bacon, Belle.'

That pleased her. She giggled, leaning close, and asked, 'Who's got a better right to save it?'

It was so dark in here that he couldn't see her face. But he could smell the cold cream she had smeared on it. Belle took good care of her skin, keeping it soft and smooth as a baby's.

A gun began blasting out back, its bullets whanging through the alley. Troop grinned. They figured he was still down there; that he could be driven out to Main Street, where other guns were waiting. He got up off the floor now, and Belle took his arm, saying, 'Come rest yourself, honey.'

Troop sank into the easy chair against the wall. 'That deal down there was close,' he mused. 'Too close for comfort.'

Belle perched on the arm of the chair, and Troop slipped his arm around her. She was all right. A man could ride many a mile without finding one half so pretty. And she'd done him a big favor throwing that fire rope out the window.

Belle laughed happily. 'Remember the last time you took me out, Lew?'

Troop chuckled. 'We had us a time that night, for a fact.'

'More fun than a cage of monkeys,' Belle agreed, giggling. 'Remember how Lon Sing tried to make me stop dancing barefoot on his lunch counter, and you threatened to cut off his pigtail?'

'Sure,' Troop said. 'I'd've done it, too.'

Someone out front shouted, 'Where the hell is Troop?'

Belle asked, 'Why were they chasing you, Lew?'

'Well, it started when I hit Lee Monroe and broke his nose.'

'Why'd you hit him?'

'Because he was running off at the mouth about Fern Borgstrom.'

'What difference did it make to you?' Belle asked.

'Well, I just didn't like the sound of it. Or Chastain telling me I couldn't work for her.'

Belle drew away from him abruptly. 'You mean you've hired out to her?'

'Yes,' Troop said. 'Start work for her tomorrow—if I can make it out there with a whole skin.'

'Well, I like that!' Belle exclaimed. 'You working for an uppity Swede who thinks she's the Queen of Sheba!' And then, as if thinking out loud, she said angrily, 'So that's what ailed you this evening! That's why you treated me like I was some jenny cat you couldn't stand to kiss!' She stood up. 'Why, you no-good tramp!' she stormed. 'Falling for an uppity Swede that wouldn't let you lay a hand on her if you begged her on bended knees!'

'Oh, for Christ's sake,' Troop said wearily.

'And after the way I practically saved your life!' Belle ranted, her voice rising to a shrill shout.

'Not so loud,' Troop cautioned. 'You'll have those bastards up here.'

'Sure I will,' Belle spat at him. 'I'll fix your piano right now!'

Then she ran toward the window, screaming, 'Sheriff Eggleston!'

Troop tried to grab her, but she slipped from his grasp and reached the open window. She shouted, 'He's up here, Bill! Troop is in my room!'

He got hold of her then. He yanked her

63

back and clamped a hand over her mouth. But the damage, he realized, was already done. 'You mouthy trollop!' he muttered. He pushed her roughly away from him. Then he turned to the door, flung it open, and ran into the dark hallway. There must be a rear stairway, he thought, and he was hurrying toward the back when the pimply-faced clerk stepped from a room with a lamp held high in one hand.

Narrowly avoiding collision, Troop rammed the muzzle of his gun against the clerk's striped nightshirt and demanded, 'Is there a back stairway?'

'Y-y-yes.'

'Lead me to it, quick,' Troop ordered.

Hearing boots on the lobby stairs, he blew out the lamp.

The barefooted clerk went along the dark corridor like a spooked jack rabbit scurrying to its burrow.

CHAPTER SIX

Joe Shedrow couldn't understand it. All that shooting and they still hadn't got Troop. With three guns going full tilt and half the town looking on, Troop had disappeared.

Vanished, by grab, as if he'd sprouted wings and flown out of Signal like a bird. He hadn't even got wounded. Leastwise, that's what folks were saying out there on Main Street. Drunk-lucky, they called him. Not a drop of blood to be seen anywhere. Three guns going. What an uproar it had been while it lasted! Shedrow hadn't seen all of it, for there'd been a chore that needed doing. But he'd heard the fight from start to finish. There was a brief lull in the shooting, then some woman had started screaming upstreet, and soon after that there'd been a hell-smear of shooting out behind the Palacial Hotel. As if they'd cornered Troop in South Alley.

Joe stood at the head of that alley now. If Troop was in there, he'd most likely come this way, wanting his horse. Signal was no place for him now. Even a devil-be-damned galoot like Troop would understand that.

Shedrow heard someone talking far down the alley, and a remote rumor of footsteps on a rear stairway. Then a dozen dogs began barking in a dozen back yards and it seemed like all the women on Grand Avenue were hollering at their dogs and menfolk to get back into their houses. What a hell-tootin' racket they made!

Joe turned up his mackinaw collar against the night's increasing coldness, and stamped his feet. Here he was with thin soles in his shoes again, and winter coming on. Just like he'd been a year ago. Shedrow sighed, recalling how sure he'd been that there would be cash aplenty before snow fell. He had dug his heart out all summer, knowing he was smack-dab close to the big cache—the Curly Bill cache. But a man couldn't haul firewood and do a proper job of digging for treasure at the same time.

Someone far up the alley shouted, 'He ain't out here, Bill.'

Where, Shedrow wondered, could Troop have gone? The durn jigger couldn't have used Main Street for a getaway. Not that Joe would put Troop past trying it. He wondered how it was that some men didn't seem to know the meaning of fear. Take Troop, for instance. He had faced up to Chastain like Dade was no better than he was; not as good, maybe. And look how he'd gone out there on Main Street, knowing Lee Monroe was gunning for him. How could a feller do a thing like that—risk getting shot when there was no need of it? As if a gun fight on a dark street was a natural thing.

That, Joe reflected, was how most cow folks seemed to be; just natural-borned fighters. Maybe it was a thing you got from sitting on a saddle, year in and year out. Must be it did something to your backbone, making it stiffer. Or maybe cowmen were just born with a special knack for fighting. Like other men were natural-borned fiddlers or guitar players, or stage actors . . .

★   ★   ★

Lew Troop had forced the barefooted clerk to accompany him down the rear stairway to a row of privies behind the hotel. Pushing his frightened guide inside one of the ill-smelling cubicles, Troop had ordered, 'Take yourself a squat and keep your goddamn mouth shut.'

Then he had cat-footed into South Alley with his spurs in one hand and his gun in the other.

Now, as Troop eased cautiously along the trash-littered lane, he had one idea in mind— to reach Ledbetter's barn. If his luck would hold long enough to get astride Blue, he could kiss this stinking town good-by. Dogs began barking behind him, and foot tromp sounded on the hotel's rear stairs. A man high up on the back gallery yelled, 'Any of you boys out there?' When there was no reply he began firing into the alley. A bullet spanged through tin cans behind Troop. A woman in the back yard of a house on Grand Avenue shrilled 'John! Where are you, John?'

Troop stumbled in a rubbish pile, and cursed a dog that yipped at him in the yonder darkness. He wondered if the pimply-faced clerk would keep his mouth shut, and guessed he might. That dude had been so spooked he couldn't talk. Troop grinned, recalling how the night-shirted clerk had stuttered, how his teeth had chattered.

There were more shots behind him. And more shouting. Sheriff Eggleston, he supposed, was getting impatient. What a goddamn counterfeit he was, that Big Bill. Ganging up on a man who'd done nothing more than stand up for his rights.

Troop wondered what Belle Smith would tell Eggleston—how she would explain his presence in her room. She couldn't admit throwing him the fire rope; Big Bill would boot her out of his hotel if she told him that. Remembering how abruptly Belle had shifted from open receptiveness to rage-prodded scorn, Troop swore softly. Women were downright unpredictable. They were chancy as the changing winds, and with no more reason for their shifting.

He was into the alleyhead when Joe Shedrow called softly, 'Is that you, Troop?'

'Yes,' Troop said. He still didn't see him, it was so dark there, until Shedrow moved.

'I tied your horse to the wagon-yard fence

right over there,' Joe said.

'Good,' Troop said. 'Good deal, friend.'

'Almost thought I was wastin' my time. Thought mebbe you'd need a coffin instead of a horse. How'd you git shut of them jiggers?'

'Went through a woman's room at the hotel,' Troop said. 'Didn't you hear her holler?'

'Say, that wasn't Belle, was it?'

'Yeah, Belle Smith, damn her!'

'She's my wife,' Shedrow interrupted.

'*Your* wife?' Troop demanded. 'Belle Smith?'

'She took back her maiden name when she quit me,' Joe explained, 'but she's still my legal wife, by grab.' Then he asked urgently, 'You didn't hurt her, did you?'

Troop loosed a long-drawn sigh. 'Just her feelings,' he said. He chuckled, thinking what a joke it was. But it wasn't comical, exactly, Belle cuddling close against him in the big chair while her husband moved his horse so it would be handy for a getaway. It made him feel ashamed, and glad he hadn't done more than hug her, or known she was Joe's wife.

'Belle will come back with me,' Shedrow said confidently. 'She just couldn't abide town poverty, is all. It got so's I couldn't even buy her a decent dress or a new pair of shoes. A pretty woman just has to have them things.

69

Life ain't worth livin' otherwise.'

A secretive tone came into his voice now as he added, 'I'll be a rich man one of these days. I'll buy her all the nice things we couldn't afford. Belle has the makin's of a mighty fine wife in more ways than one. I'm glad she got out of that danged dance hall. That's no place for a high-class woman like her.'

'That's right,' Troop agreed, and he was embarrassed by this man's loyalty to a woman who had so eagerly transferred her affections to a fiddle-footed drifter. By God, it was pitiful when you stopped to think of it; Joe eating his heart out while his wife trifled with other men. Troop wondered if Belle had called Joe 'honey,' and felt a trifle sick at his stomach as Shedrow walked over to the wagon-shed fence with him.

Women! By God, you could have the whole deceitful bunch of them!

Afterward, when Troop had crossed Canteen Creek, he made camp on a timbered hill. There was a raw dampness in the night air now, and a rising wind stirred the high pines to restless sighing. Rolled in a blanket with his boots on, Troop thought about Joe Shedrow—how the nester had shaken hands at parting and promised to help, any way he could. As if he hadn't already helped aplenty, warning of Monroe's ambush and all. . .

'He probably saved my life,' Troop muttered, and again felt a nagging sense of shame.

★　　★　　★

Belle Smith closed her front window with a bang. Those loud-mouthed fools on the hotel veranda would wag their jaws till daylight, talking about Lew Troop. Damn him! she thought, and was about to blow out the lamp when Sheriff Eggleston walked into the room.

'You're supposed to knock,' Belle protested, backing away from him. 'You shouldn't just walk into a girl's room.'

Eggleston closed the door behind him. He took off his hat and asked, 'How did Troop get up here, Belle?'

She shrugged. 'How in heaven's name would I know? He just walked in, same as you did.'

'Can't figger it out,' Eggleston muttered, his yellowish brown eyes appraising her. 'We had him boxed in the alley.'

Belle lifted a hand to brush back a vagrant strand of hair. 'I called out, didn't I?' she said. 'What more could I do?'

'That's right,' Big Bill agreed. He reached out and patted her shoulder. 'You did just right.'

Then he grabbed her with both hands and brought her hard against him. 'Belle, sweetheart!' he exclaimed, and tried to kiss her.

'You're hurting me!' Belle cried, bracing her hands against him. 'Let me go!'

Eggleston laughed, and lifting her clear of the floor, turned toward the bed. 'You been holdin' me off long enough,' he chuckled. 'A man can stand just so much teasin'.'

Belle squirmed; her silk-clad body slipped through his embracing arms and she dodged away, protesting, 'No, Bill—no!'

'Why not?' he demanded, following as she circled just out of reach. 'I took you out of that dance hall, didn't I? You like me, don't you?'

'Sure,' Belle said, backtracking as she talked. 'Sure I do. I like you just fine.'

'Then how about showing it, girl?'

Belle shook her head. 'I can't—not like that. It wouldn't be fitting, until Joe gives me a divorce.'

That stopped Big Bill in his tracks. He stared at her, his mouth slack-jawed with puzzlement. 'You mean you ain't been with a man since you quit Shedrow?'

Belle nodded.

'None of them free-spending dance-hall bucks?' the sheriff asked disbelievingly.

'Of course not,' Belle said. Seeing the

baffled expression on his face, she gave him a haughty, indignant look. 'What do you take me for?'

Big Bill ran a hand across his perspiring face. 'It beats me,' he muttered, gawking at her as if she were someone he'd never seen before. 'It sure does. I thought you was just givin' me a come-on; just actin' hard to get. I figgered you was a triflin' woman holdin' out just to tease me.'

'Good gracious—how can you say such things!' Belle exclaimed. 'How could you think a thing like that about me?' She seemed on the verge of tears. Righteous indignation throbbed in her low voice as she demanded, 'How ever could you, Bill Eggleston?'

Then she pushed him toward the door, and could scarcely keep from laughing when Big Bill said, 'I should of knowed different. I'm sure sorry, Belle. I certainly am.'

He turned in the doorway and asked meekly, 'You believe that, don't you, girl—about me bein' sorry?'

'Sorry because I'm not a trifling woman?' Belle inquired with pouting gravity.

'No—yes. I mean, I'm sorry I insulted you,' Eggleston mumbled in blushing confusion. 'I really am, girl.'

Belle couldn't look at him and keep a straight face. He was that comical. She said,

'All right, but don't ever do it again.'

She closed the door and locked it, and was doubled over with laughter as she put out the lamp. What a fool Eggleston was! What a ladies' man! She was still laughing when she got into bed.

'I'm sorry, girl,' she mocked joyously. I certainly am.'

But presently she got to thinking about Lew Troop, and how he'd gone haywire over Fern Borgstrom; over a woman he hadn't even kissed. Gone so romantic he couldn't even be nice to a girl who'd give him anything he wanted.

'Damn men,' she whispered sobbingly. 'Damn them all!'

CHAPTER SEVEN

A solid bank of low, lead-gray clouds obscured the sun as Lew Troop rode down the slope toward Borgstrom's place an hour after dawn. A cold wind ran off the hills and frost made a white lace across the Free Strip flats. This, Troop thought glumly, was how winter came to Cathedral Basin: warm one day and cold the next. Might be snowing tomorrow.

He had awakened shivering, and was still

stiff-bodied with cold. The taste of last night's bourbon was bitter in his mouth. He imagined he could also taste the greasy cream Belle Smith had smeared on her face. By God, he'd been a fool in more ways than one. A man that stupid should quit booze and women both. He should keep his mouth shut and his backtrail open. But he'd made his big brag in public, and there was no chance of ducking this deal. If Fern Borgstrom still wanted a hired man, he was it.

Troop shivered, shrugged deeper into his brush jacket, and muttered morosely, 'I talked us into a session with the snowballs, Blue.'

When he approached the Borgstrom cabin Troop wondered why no smoke showed above the rusty stovepipe. Fern should be up by now. Homesteader women were supposed to be an early-rising bunch. And good cooks, when they had food to cook. There was a hunger grind in Troop's belly now. He had hoped there'd be hot coffee and an invitation to breakfast. But she didn't even have a fire going. He crossed the weed-grown garden and noticed that the cabin door was open, which seemed odd for so cold a morning.

Abruptly then Troop guessed what had happened. Dade Chastain hadn't waited until the noon deadline. Believing Fern Borgstrom

75

had hired a man to defend her rights, the Slash C boss had decided on a surprise visit at first daylight.

Thought they'd catch me asleep, Troop reflected, and presently studied the tracks in front of the cabin. Two riders had accompanied a wagon out of the yard. The tracks were fresh, with manure so recently dropped there was no frost on it. Not more than half an hour old, Troop calculated. Which meant he could easily overtake the wagon before it reached town. But why should he?

Troop grinned. He had kept his word, hadn't he? He'd done what he'd said he would do. It wasn't his fault if there was no job here for him!

'By God, we're going south!' Troop told his horse. 'We're heading for the desert!'

He wondered if the two riders would escort Fern Borgstrom all the way to town, or just to the stage road. Not that it made any difference. He would give Signal a wide berth, not wanting to see Chastain's riders or the sorrel-haired woman. He wondered if she had put up a struggle, and was sure she had been forcibly evicted. She wouldn't have left, otherwise.

'Hell of a deal,' he muttered, and now noticed the frilly white curtains that adorned both front windows.

That was a woman for you. Come hell or high water, they had to fix things fancy. The curtains seemed completely at odds with the dilapidated cabin, ramshackle barn, and rubbish-littered yard. They were like futile symbols of graciousness against the forlorn reality of this abandoned place.

Troop took out his Durham sack and put his cold fingers to shaping a cigarette. There might have been a chance of bluffing it out with those Slash C riders if he had been here. Dade Chastain knew how to handle clumsy sodbusters, who seldom used guns, but he wouldn't be so confident against one of his own kind. He had shown that last night in the saloon. Dade hadn't been quite sure. And he might have felt the same way here this morning. But it was too late now, Troop thought, and took pleasure in the realization that he was free of the loco fix he'd got himself into last night. He thumbed a match aflame and was shielding it against the wind with both palms when Dade Chastain called, 'Sit still, bronc-stomper—real still!'

Caught completely unprepared, Troop turned to see Chastain standing in the cabin doorway with a gun in his hand.

'Put up your hands,' Chastain ordered, 'where I can see them both.'

77

For a fleeting moment Troop considered making a play. If he yanked back on the reins and Blue reared, there might be a chance of shooting this out with Chastain.

Then, realizing how little chance there would be, he raised his hands shoulder-high. A man might better wait for a real chance. He watched Chastain walk toward him, and wondered where Dade's horse was hidden. There'd been no greeting whinny. Chastain's grave face showed neither satisfaction nor anticipation; nothing beyond a wary intentness. If there was any real emotion in Dade Chastain, he kept it well concealed. The man was like a precision-geared machine that never varied its exact turning or failed in a prescribed efficiency.

'Thought you would show eventually,' Chastain said. 'You drifters are always an hour late and a dollar short.'

He came up on Troop's right side, keeping the cocked pistol aimed at Troop's belt buckle as he lifted Troop's gun from its holster and tossed it away. Then he said, 'Get down, bronc-stomper. We'll go into the cabin and wait for Monk and Oak Creek.'

Swift understanding came to Troop at mention of those names. A tight knot of apprehension formed at the pit of his stomach, and he thought, So that's how it's going to be!

78

Monk Monroe could knock a horse to its knees with one chopping blow of his right fist. Lee's brother had a reputation as an accomplished rough-and-tumble fighter, and so did Oak Creek Kirby. But Monk, who'd have heard what happened to Lee, would be the one . . .

Troop got down, grimacing at the stiffness of his cold-numbed legs. This was what getting drunk in town did to a man; this was how you paid for a little session with booze and women. By God, the church folks had the right of it, he decided, about sinners having to pay off. He hadn't had much fun last night, but he'd paid aplenty for it, and would pay more.

Chastain motioned for him to go into the cabin. He said sarcastically. 'You should feel right at home, being a nester lover.'

Troop moved slowly into the doorway, hoping that Dade would come close enough so there'd be a chance to whirl and grab his gun arm. But Chastain spoiled that by ramming the gun's snout against his back and prodding him inside.

A saddled horse stood in one corner, barricaded by a homemade table and barrel chair. So that's why there was no whinny, Troop thought, and grudgingly gave Chastain his due. The man figured out all the angles, and was clever doing it. Who else but Dade Chastain would have thought about bringing a horse inside?

The Slash C boss motioned him to a blanketless bunk, then sat himself down in the barrel chair. He said, 'You talked real tough in town last night. Like you just didn't give a damn, regardless. Don't recollect ever hearing a man talk any tougher. But you act tame enough now.'

Troop shrugged. He took out his Durham sack, built a cigarette, and smoked it in silence. Talk had got him into this, but it wouldn't get him out. He could talk his goddamn heart out for all the good it would do. No man stood up to Dade Chastain as he'd done last night and got any mercy. The word wasn't in Dade's book at all. He probably couldn't even spell it.

Except for the white curtains at the windows, there wasn't a thing to show that Fern Borgstrom had spent the night here. The stove was cold; no sign of a dish or morsel of food. He wondered how it had been for her last night, alone here with memories of her dead father, thinking of all the lonely nights he'd spent in this cabin. All the fearful nights. It must have been bad for her. She probably hadn't slept much, thinking about Swede, and being evicted. Perhaps it was so bad she hadn't minded leaving. This place wasn't much to look at when the sun was shining; it must have looked sorry to her on a cold gloomy morning.

She'll probably go back to teaching school in Texas, Troop thought. And because he couldn't discard the memory of her warm blue eyes, he wondered if he might meet up with her again sometime.

Wind-blown rain spattered against the front windows. Cold air came through the faulty chinking, filling the cabin with a chill dampness. When Troop put his hands into his pockets Chastain said, 'Keep them there,' and holstered his gun. He lit a cigar and had it smoked half down before he said, 'Swede's daughter is uncommon pretty for a nester woman. But I still don't see how she talked you into such a damn-fool deal.'

'She didn't,' Troop corrected. 'You're the one that talked me into it.'

'Me?' Chastain demanded. 'What did I have to do with it?'

'You tried to spook me out of town, same as you have so many others,' Troop explained. 'Well, I don't spook.'

That didn't seem to make sense to Dade Chastain. 'I just told you to keep away from the Free Strip, was all,' he argued. 'Why should that make you want to work for Miss

Borgstrom?'

'You wouldn't understand it,' Troop muttered. 'But I'll tell you something, Chastain. You may be able to browbeat Kansas farmers, or even some cowboys from different parts of the country. But don't ever try pushing Texas men around. We don't take it. We may get hell whipped out of us occasionally, but we won't be pushed around, regardless.'

Chastain snorted. 'What kind of damn-fool talk is that?' he demanded. 'Just because a saddle bum hails from Texas doesn't make him any better. A shiftless bum is a shiftless bum no matter where he was born. And he gets pushed around. It's always been that way, and it always will be. I told you to stay away from here, which was my right. But you had to act smart-alecky for the benefit of those saloon loafers. Now, by God, you're going to pay for it.'

'How?' Troop asked, urgently curious to know what Chastain had in mind.

'You'll find out when the time comes,' Dade said. He tossed his smoked-out cigar at the stove and muttered, 'It's getting awful cold in here. Reckon you'd better build up a fire.'

Troop was on the verge of telling him to go to hell—that if he wanted a fire he could build it himself. But the fingers of his right hand had been fiddling with his jackknife, and now it occurred to him that making a fire might give him a chance to try changing this setup. If he could get close enough to Chastain, who sat near the stove . . .

He got off the bunk, walked over to the woodbox, and picked up a piece of kindling. Borgstrom's stove was a rusty old wood-burning range with an oven in its middle and a water tank on its tail end. Troop lifted the lid and peered down into the grate, where a few live coals still gave a feeble glow.

'Plumb out,' he said, replacing the lid, and now saw that Chastain had drawn his gun.

'Just in case you get any foolish ideas,' Dade announced.

Troop shrugged. The stiff-backed bastard wasn't taking any chances. None at all. Troop took out his knife and began slicing thin shavings from the pine stick. There were some heavier pieces of sawed pine in the woodbox. They were just the right length for fast, close-up swinging. But that goddamn gun . . .

Whittling industriously, Troop was aware of Chastain's watchful eyes. The Slash C boss was as alert as a man could be. If it was Sheriff Eggleston now, or Monk Monroe, there might be a chance. Then a new idea came to him, and he thought, It might work. It just might!

'Haven't you got enough shavings?' Chastain asked impatiently.

'Who's building this fire?' Troop muttered, and kept on with the knife.

Presently Chastain said, 'Come on, come on. You've got more'n enough. Let's get a fire going.'

Even then Troop whittled a few more shavings before he went to the stove, took the lid off again, and poked around in the ashes with what remained of the pine stick.

'Maybe you'd better do a stove-blacking job also, before you build that fire,' Chastain jibed.

Troop frowned at him. 'I like a proper draft in a stove,' he said.

Then he scooped up the big pile of shavings in both hands and, whirling abruptly, flung them into Chastain's face.

The barrel chair went over backward as Chastain dodged. The gun went off as Troop grabbed Dade's right arm, the muzzle flame so close it scorched Troop's sleeve. He got both hands on Chastain's arm and swung completely around with him as the gun exploded twice. He forced Chastain against the back wall, and heard a continuing commotion behind him as he fought to keep the gun pointed away from him. Dade's horse, he guessed, had got spooked by the shooting and was trying to kick his way out of the cabin.

Chastain kept stabbing at Troop's unprotected face with his left hand; kept endeavoring to bring that gun barrel down. Troop lifted a knee and drove it into Chastain's crotch, and felt his arm go limp. Dade loosed a rasping groan. He let go of the gun and grabbed himself with both hands and shrilled, 'Goddamn you, Troop!'

Picking up the gun, Troop backed off and glanced at Chastain's bay gelding. The horse was spraddled out on its side, one hind leg twitching convulsively. A pool of blood was already forming on the rammed earth floor.

'You shot your own horse,' Troop said.

Chastain straightened up. His lean, high-beaked face was a trifle pale. But even now, feeling pain and anger as he must be, Dade showed no visible emotion. 'My mistake,' he admitted in his cool, precise voice. 'My mistake having you build the fire, also.'

By God, you had to hand it to him, Troop reflected. He was a cold potato that just never got hot.

'I'll give the orders now,' Troop said, gesturing with the gun. 'Scramble up those shavings and put 'em in the stove.'

Rain was pelting hard against the roof, making a drum-beat of steady sound. Half sleet, Troop thought, by the clatter of it. Chastain had scooped up the shavings and was turning toward the stove when he stopped in mid-stride. His eyes, Troop thought, looked like bright blue marbles. They had a queer shine to them.

At this same moment he became aware of cold damp air against the back of his neck and knew the door was open. That was when Monk Monroe called triumphantly, 'We got two guns aimed at your backbone, Troop!'

CHAPTER EIGHT

They had him. If he'd had the slightest doubt of it, the exultation Lew Troop saw in Chastain's eyes would have banished it. Dade dropped the shavings at once. He said, 'You had your turn giving the orders, now I'll give them. Lay that gun on the table.'

When Troop hesitated for a moment longer, Oak Creek Kirby said, 'Step to one side, boss, and we'll let him have it.'

Troop put the gun on the table. He turned around and looked at the two men who stood in dripping yellow slickers with guns in their wet hands. Monk's broad, ape-featured face held an expansive grin, and there was a tight expectancy in Oak Creek's deep-socketed eyes. Kirby, Troop thought, looked like a hunger-gaunted coyote smelling raw meat.

'So you turned nester lover,' Monk scoffed, 'and slugged my brother Lee.'

Chastain picked up his gun and holstered it and asked, 'Did you escort Miss Borgstrom across Canteen Creek?'

'Yeah,' Monroe said, the grin ruts deepening in his whisker-bristled cheeks. 'I offered to keep her company all the way to town, but she wasn't the least bit sociable.'

Swift anger flamed in Chastain's eyes. 'I told you there was to be no rudeness,' he snapped.

That astonished Lew Troop. It seemed like a monstrous joke. No rudeness! Coming from a man who'd forcibly evicted a defenseless woman from her home, it seemed as comical as the senseless mouthings of a circus clown.

'I was just funnin' with her,' Monk explained. 'That woman is colder'n sixteen icicles in a cave.'

Oak Creek still held his gun. He asked, 'What we goin' to do with him, boss?'

'He's Monk's meat, like I promised,' Chastain said. 'Knuckle meat.'

Monroe took off his slicker and rolled up his sleeves, exposing forearms big as freighter wheel hubs. He glanced at the dead horse and asked, 'How'd the bay git shot?'

'Accidentally, of course,' Chastain said. 'You see Troop's horse outside?' And when Monk nodded, Dade said, 'Take my saddle off the bay, Oak Creek, and put it on the grulla.'

Troop didn't like that at all. He said, 'You shot the horse yourself, Chastain. You've got no right to mine.'

A calculating sharpness came into Chastain's milk-blue eyes. 'You think a lot of that grulla, don't you, Troop?' he said thoughtfully.

'Raised him from a limber-legged colt,' Troop muttered. 'I'm the only one who's ever rode him.'

Monroe laughed. He said, 'Well, mebbe you won't be in no shape to ride when I git through with you.'

He hunched his sloping shoulders, loosening them, and started forward. But Chastain said, 'Hold up a minute, Monk.' Then he turned to Troop, saying, 'You wouldn't want the grulla choused around by a hard-handed man, would you? Say, by someone like Monk, who has no patience with a horse?'

'No,' Troop said. 'I wouldn't.'

Chastain came as near to smiling then as Troop had ever seen him. Dade said, 'Like I told you yesterday, I'm real short-handed. It looks like we'll be getting snow any day now, and I'd stand to lose a lot of cattle if they got caught up there in the Rimrocks. So I'll make you a little proposition, Troop. You ride with us for one week, and the grulla is yours.'

The unexpectedness of that proposition bewildered Lew Troop. What the hell was Chastain driving at? He said, 'Blue is mine already.'

'No,' Chastain said. 'I'm riding him away from here, and you'll have to earn him back.'

Troop shook his head. 'I'll do no riding for you,' he muttered. 'Not by a damned sight.'

Chastain shrugged. He turned to Monroe and said, 'You'll be riding the grulla on the gather, Monk.'

'Good,' Monroe agreed. He smirked at Troop, predicting, 'I'll ride his goddamn legs off, I'll chouse him through them rocks till there'll be nothin' left but bleedin' stumps.'

And so he would, Troop realized with sickening surety. Monroe was a spur-gouging hellion with horses; a red-rowel brute. And he'd be merciless with Blue, just for spite. It was enough to make a man's flesh crawl, just to think of it. Remembering all the miles he'd ridden Blue, all the lonely campfires they'd shared and the times they'd drunk from the same water hole, cheek to cheek, Troop cursed whisperingly. Blue had a mouth like velvet; a sweet, soft mouth that had never been abused by curb-bit punishment. And a big-hearted courage that would keep him going until he dropped. To have such a horse ruined by a bastard like Monroe...

Troop turned to Chastain. He said with shrugging resignation, 'You win. I'll work with the gather—for one week.'

'Fine!' the Slash C boss said. 'That's fine. Oak Creek will leave you his horse, and we'll ride double to the ranch. You be out there by daylight tomorrow morning, which is when we'll be starting for the roughs.'

That puzzled Troop. It sounded like they were going to leave him here. But why?

Then, as Monroe asked eagerly, 'Shall I give it to him now?' Troop understood. Monk had been promised his pound of vengeance flesh.

Chastain nodded. 'Make it fast. We've got work to do at the ranch.'

Troop backed toward the center of the room as Monroe advanced, waggling his fists. Monk, he supposed, outweighed him by thirty pounds or more. The ape-faced rider was built like a barrel, with scarcely any neck at all.

'I'll learn you to slug my brother!' Monroe snarled, and lunged forward.

Troop side-stepped, narrowly evading the big man's two-fisted attack, and now Oak Creek asked, 'Want me to haze him for you?'

Kirby came quickly around, forcing Troop so that he collided with the bunk and sat down. Monroe was already charging again with a hot eagerness in his eyes. He snarled. 'Now you git your needin's!'

Troop waited until Monroe was almost on him before he moved. Then he came off the bunk in a sidewise spring and pivoted, catching Monroe so completely off balance that he hit him twice before Monk's guarding arms came up.

Momentarily dazed, Monroe crashed into the bunk. Troop grasped his shoulder and swung him around for a knockout punch. But before his cocked fist had a target, Oak Creek tackled Troop from behind. His clawing hands came around Troop chest-high, locking Lew's arms in a bear hug that rendered him helpless. Unable to tear loose, Troop stomped one of Kirby's feet with a boot heel. Oak Creek uttered a pain-prodded yelp, but his clamping arms remained vise-tight and he shouted, 'What you waitin' on, Monk?'

Monroe came up with both fists cocked. His lips peeled back from yellowed teeth and he snarled, 'You smart-alecky bastard!'

He measured with his left. He drove his

91

right fist into Troop's face with a wicked, full-armed swing. A groan slid from Troop's smashed lips and Oak Creek shouted gleefully, 'You made him squawk!'

Monroe hit Troop again, and getting no sound from Lew's locked lips, he snarled, 'Squawk some more, nester lover!'

Troop kept struggling to free himself of Kirby's arms. He tried to give with the blows that now came, jolt on crushing jolt. But Kirby was propped solidly behind him, allowing no more than an inch of movement.

'You've had your fun,' Chastain announced from across the room. 'Get it done with.'

Troop didn't see the blow that knocked him down. Groggy now, and gasping for breath, he clung to a fragile strand of consciousness. He was blindly propping himself to get up when Monroe stepped on his left hand, mashing his fingers into the rammed-earth floor. The sheer pain of that made Troop gasp and he was remotely aware of Oak Creek saying, 'He ain't out yet.'

Then something exploded against Troop's left ear.

Afterward, as if from a far distance, Troop heard Dade Chastain say, 'He'll come for his horse. You can depend on that.'

And then, for a time, there was nothing at all . . .

CHAPTER NINE

Fern Borgstrom's wagon was within a hundred yards of the front gate when she caught a rain-fogged glimpse of two slicker-draped shapes moving out of the yard. Halting her team instantly, she watched them merge with the meadow's misty, dusklike gloom, hugely thankful that they had not noticed her.

She made a forlorn sight, sitting there on the rain-pelted wagon wearing a floppy-brimmed hat and an old overcoat retrieved from her father's belongings. A dripping, water-soaked, lonely sight. But because she possessed a certain secret knowledge—or believed she did—Fern Borgstrom's return to her homestead was motivated by more than what Sheriff Eggleston had called 'Swede stubbornness.' It was a subtle thing, this knowledge; a thing so secret and elusive that few women would have detected it. But then, of course, few women would have placed themselves in a position to recognize what she had observed.

Now, as Fern drove into the yard, she saw a bay horse standing at the corral fence with its back humped against the cold rain. Nearby was an upended saddle. That, she decided, meant that one man had remained in the cabin.

Which one?

She remembered that Chastain had ridden a bay horse, and so had one of his men. The small man.

Fern had supposed that Chastain would ride back to his ranch while the two Slash C riders escorted her to Canteen Creek. But he evidently hadn't. Yet what possible reason could he have for waiting here? Chastain wouldn't have guessed she'd be back; that her seeming acquiescence had been prompted by the knowledge that she would come back a dozen times if necessary. Or had he?

Shrugging off that question, Fern drove up in front of the cabin, wrapped the lines around the brake handle, and got down. If Dade Chastain *had* guessed she might be back, his being here now could mean but one thing—he wanted to be alone with her.

That possibility caused Fern to hesitate with her hand on the latch. She called, 'Who's in there?' and waited a long moment before opening the door. Then, as the door swung inward, she saw Lew Troop's sprawled body.

What was he doing here?

When had he come?

Lew Troop was the last person she had expected to see here. Going south, he'd said;

couldn't stand cold weather.

He was lying on his back with blood dribbling from both nostrils. There was an ugly bruise on one jaw and a gash above his right eye. He looked, she thought, as if he'd been clubbed to death. For a fear-prodded instant Fern thought he *was* dead, so still and lifeless he looked. Then she saw his battered lips twitch and observed the gentle lifting and lowering of his chest as he breathed.

There was a bucket of water on the bench beside the door. Fern was reaching for it when she noticed the dead horse. 'Good heavens!' she exclaimed, feeling a woman's revulsion at sight of a great pool of blood on the floor. This barren room had seemed gloomy enough when she left it a couple of hours ago; now it had the grisly aspects of a slaughterhouse.

Picking up the bucket, Fern sluiced its contents upon Troop's face. Then she knelt beside him and urged, 'Wake up, Mr. Troop! Wake up!'

Troop grunted. He opened his eyes, and blinked, and peered dazedly up at her. He shook his head, as if disbelieving what he saw, and demanded, 'What you doing here?'

Fern smiled. 'I could ask you the same question,' she suggested. 'Is—is anything broken?'

Troop sat up. He looked at the mashed

flesh on his fingers and said solemnly, 'The bastards. The dirty, stinking bastards.'

Then he flexed his fingers, felt of his bloody nose, and announced, 'Nothing broken. Just badly bent, is all.'

Fern glanced at the dead horse. 'Yours?'

Troop shook his head. 'Chastain took mine.'

'There's another horse at the corral,' Fern reported.

'Oak Creek Kirby's,' Troop muttered.

When he got up, Fern rose with him, so that they stood a foot apart, peering at each other in silence until he grinned and said, 'So Chastain didn't run you off after all.'

'He will never run me off,' Fern said quietly. She reached up and explored the gash on his forehead with a gentle finger and said, 'I have a medicine kit in the wagon.'

When she went out to get it Troop walked over to the table and looked at the bay's death-stiffened carcass. How, he wondered, would they get it out of here? If the bay had fallen near the center of the room it would have been fairly simple to drag him through the doorway. But not from this angle.

Fern came in with her medicine kit. Her fingers, Troop observed, were wet and red. She looked as if she were soaked to the skin despite the overcoat.

'I'll build up a fire,' he offered.

But Fern said, 'It can wait,' and opened the medicine kit.

Afterward, when she had administered first aid, and Troop had a fire going, she asked, 'Did you have breakfast?'

'No,' Troop said. 'Planned on having it here—with you.'

That seemed to please her, for she smiled and announced, 'I'll have food on the table in a jiffy.'

While Fern secured cooking utensils and food supplies from the wagon, Troop went out and searched for his gun. There was a clutching soreness in his stomach muscles so that when he bent down to retrieve the Walker Model Colt he loosed a low groan. His upper body, he supposed, was a mass of bruises. That Monk Monroe hit hard. God-awful hard.

Troop went to the corral, took his coiled rope off the saddle, and went back to the cabin, where he proceeded to hog-tie the bay's hind feet. Fern, busy at the stove, asked, 'How will you manage it?'

'Haven't got it figured out yet,' Troop admitted. He stood for a moment, calculating the angle of pull and knowing the rope wouldn't stand it. The strands would fray out against the doorframe. 'Wish Swede had put a window at the west end,' he said.

'It would be simple.'

Fern looked at the unbroken log wall. She asked, 'If the chinking between the second and third logs was taken out, wouldn't the rope go through?'

'Hell, yes!' Troop exclaimed. He nudged back his hat and eyed her with frank admiration and asked, 'Now, why didn't I think of that?'

'Because you are not a homesteader,' Fern said smilingly. 'You do your thinking on horseback.'

Even so, with a straight pull, it was quite a chore. The team slipped and floundered in the yard's hoof-deep mud. But by dint of Troop's patient coaxing, with Fern calling instructions, the bay's carcass was dragged forward until it was opposite the doorway. Then, with a straightaway pull, and Fern managing the team while Troop propped the dead bay on its back, they got it through the doorway.

Troop took over the lines then, dragging the carcass far out across the rain-swept meadow. Then he turned the team into the corral along with Kirby's rat-tailed bay. There was a stack of old hay in the corral and half as much more stored in the high-roofed wagon shed. Swede, he reflected, had made a sort of harvest after all; a harvest that might be valuable if Fern spent the winter here. And it looked, by God, as if she might.

He was stowing his wet saddle in the shed when she called, 'Breakfast is ready!'

That was how they had their first meal together, these two stubborn ones who wouldn't be dominated. With wind-slanted rain pelting the front windows of a room that even a warm stove didn't make cheerful; with blood smeared all across the rammed-earth floor, and water, dripping from a leaky roof, forming three separate puddles.

For the first few moments at the table, Troop ate in the eager fashion of a man half starved. Now, with a generous portion of bacon, fried potatoes, and hot biscuits inside him and a second cup of coffee before him, Troop said, 'Part of that wagon shed could be fixed up for a bunkhouse, with a hammer and some nails.'

'I have a hammer and nails in the wagon,' Fern said. 'Also a sharp saw.' Then she asked, 'Have you decided to take the job?'

That question astonished Lew Troop, and angered him. What in hell did she think he had come here for—just to get his goddamn head beat off? After he'd spent half the night dodging bullets and near froze his rump off getting here, she wanted to know if he'd made a decision—a damn-fool decision that had already cost him a good horse!

He felt like giving her a piece of his mind. But he just nodded, and observed the subtle change in her blue eyes—a steady, searching appraisal that reminded him of the calculating scrutiny Chastain had given him in the saloon last night. As if she weren't quite sure about him, and needed to be sure.

'Well?' he demanded rankly. 'Is something puzzling you?'

She nodded, and now the half-smiling expression warmed her high-boned cheeks and a slow smile curved her lips. One arched eyebrow lifted in quizzical fashion and she asked, 'Isn't it a trifle odd that a man who dislikes snow should change his mind overnight?'

'Odd is right,' Troop admitted in a bitter, self-mocking tone. 'By God, I should have my brains inspected for blow flies.'

Then, because he wanted her to know why he had come back, Troop told her what had happened in the Shamrock. 'Reckon I was a trifle drunk,' he explained. 'But I can't abide being run off like a spooked sheepherder. It rubs a man the wrong way—makes him do loco things. If you want a hired man for a month, I'm it.'

Fern liked that, and showed it in the way she smiled at him; in the way she said, 'Good!'

'But I can't start work until a week from tomorrow,' Troop muttered, and then told her about the deal he'd made with Chastain. 'I couldn't stand to think of Blue being abused like that,' he explained, endeavoring to make it sound matter-of-fact, and not quite succeeding.

Fern smiled. She said, 'So,' as if sure of something now that she had only suspected before.

'So what?' Troop asked, resenting the notion that she might think he was overly soft about Blue.

Fern shrugged. 'It's just something I say when I'm thinking,' she explained. 'My father had the same habit.' Then she asked, 'Would you consider me overly bold if I call you Lew?'

'Not any,' Troop assured her. And presently, helping tote household goods into the cabin, he said, 'This is the first time I ever had a boss named Fern.'

She peered at him appraisingly and said, 'I don't suppose you ever really had a boss by any name.'

Troop thought about that as he repaired the roof, and later when he went to work with hammer and saw in the wagon shed. He had worked for a lot of men in a hell-smear of places, but he'd never taken much bossing.

Maybe that was why he hadn't got ahead in the cow business. He hadn't followed the pattern, which called for a rider to work at one ranch long enough to get a ramrod job; to save his wages and buy himself a little jag of cows. A man couldn't do that without being bossed considerable.

He grinned, remembering what his father had once told him. 'A man has to learn how to take orders before he's capable of giving them.' His old daddy had once been a foreman at the X.I.T., biggest ranch in Texas.

And I'm handy man for a woman homesteader, Troop thought glumly. It sure beat hell how haywire a man could go.

Occasionally cursing nails fumbled because of the clumsiness of his bandaged fingers, Troop spent the afternoon constructing a reasonably weatherproof room. Lacking lumber for a door, he hung a discarded tarp across the entrance, then brought a cot and bedding from the wagon.

Renegade's Roost, he named it, and took pride in what he had accomplished. Fern, who seemed to think a riding man wasn't much account afoot, might think differently when she saw this bunk room.

It was dusk, with the rain turning to sleet, when Troop fed the horses. A raw, cold wind ran off the Sun Dance Hills and the smell of impending winter was like an odor in the damp air—a dismal, unwelcome odor that made Lew Troop shiver. This country would be a miserable place once the snow set in. Crossing the rain-puddled yard, he was aware of a nagging sense of foreboding. It was probably snowing up there on the Rimrocks right now. Working cattle in this weather would be hell.

Stomping mud from his boots, Troop went into the cabin. For a moment, as his eyes focused to the lamplight, he stood there and peered about the room, marveling at what he saw. A high-chimneyed lamp with a polished brass bowl stood on the homemade table, which was now covered by a bright red-and-white checked oilcloth. A large, multicolored rag rug adorned the rammed-earth floor. A rocking chair stood in front of the double-decker bunks, which were hidden by a frilly drape that had been tacked to a rafter.

'Does it look different?' Fern asked, retrieving a pan of biscuits from the oven.

'Different?' Troop said. 'Why, it doesn't look like the same place at all.'

Remembering how cattle had used this cabin for shelter—how barren and ugly it had seemed a few hours ago—Troop could scarcely believe his eyes. It just didn't seem possible that one woman could contrive so many changes in so short a time. She had even put scalloped paper borders along the shelves above the sink. Everywhere he looked there was evidence of a woman's knack for fancy things.

'It even smells different,' Troop reflected.

'Perhaps it's the moth balls that were in the trunks,' Fern suggested.

But Troop shook his head. 'No, and it's not food. It's something else.'

And then, as she passed him on her way to the table, Lew Troop understood what it was: the scent of her sorrel hair combined with some delicate perfume that clung to her clothing.

Woman smell, Troop thought, and was astonished at what it did to him; at the way it warmed and roused him. As if he hadn't been close to a woman for six months. Remembering how it was with Belle Smith last night, how old and shrunk-up and dehorned he'd felt, Troop felt like laughing. He wasn't old now, by God!

'Aren't you hungry?' Fern asked.

'Yeah,' Troop said, and turning to the sink, he thought, In more ways than one. Gingerly washing his bruised face, he marveled at how much better he felt. Not an ache or a pain. What a woman she was, to have that effect on a man! What a wife she'd make!

But when he combed his hair, Troop frowned at the mirrored reflection of his battered face and told himself, Don't be a goddamn fool. One month of homestead chores will be aplenty.

Troop didn't tell her that the supper was the best he'd ever eaten. A man had to play it careful with a woman like Fern Borgstrom. He had to watch his step or he'd end up offering her a wedding ring. She'd be no pushover. Belle Smith, who'd probably no more than glanced at her, had understood that. It was an odd thing about women, how they could size up another woman smack-dab, just by looking at her. A man had to fuss around, had to make his try, before he knew. But a woman could tell about another woman every time.

Finished with his supper, Troop smoked a cigarette in relaxed comfort while Fern cleared off the table. She wasn't much of a talker, which suited him fine. That was the trouble with most women. They wagged their jaws too much. She had a nice, smooth way of moving. Her hips, ample enough but not bulky, swayed a little when she walked, and so did her high breasts.

When she put a dishpan of water on the stove to heat, Troop got up and reached for his hat. 'Reckon I'll turn in,' he said. 'Got to make an early start for Slash C.'

'Let me change that bandage on your hand, first,' Fern said. Then, as if aware of his continuing appraisal, she asked, 'Is something wrong with my dress?'

Troop shook his head. 'Just thinking how—how nice it looked,' he lied, and grinned at her.

'I made it myself,' she said, frankly pleased by his praise. 'This is the first time I've worn it.'

Lew Troop wasn't thinking about the dress as she doctored his bruised fingers. He was thinking about the woman in the dress; he was smelling the feminine fragrance of her and seeing how her sorrel hair shone in the lamplight. He had a prodding impulse to touch her hair, to rumple it, so that she wouldn't look so prim and proper. He looked at her moist full lips and tantalized himself with wondering how it would be to kiss them.

'Do you think there's any danger of Chastain's men coming back while you're gone?' she asked.

'Not any,' Troop said. 'They'll all be up in the roughs chousing cattle. Chastain is worried about getting them out before a big snow comes. He won't bother you for at least a week. He won't even know you're here.'

Afterward, pulling off his boots in the

lantern-lit bunk room, Troop kept thinking about her lips. They'd be like soft cushions against a man's mouth.

Then he wondered what the hell had got into him, thinking about a kiss like some slick-eared youngster making his first sashay with a girl. That beating, he guessed, must have turned him a trifle loco in the head. A man might succeed in kissing Fern Borgstrom, but that was all he'd get.

He would have to be asaddle long before daybreak. Chastain, he supposed, would push the crew from dawn till dark. He'd want two days' work done in one, regardless of the weather. It would be a tedious way for a man to get back a horse he already owned. It occurred to him that there might be an easier, quicker way, with a gun. And a little luck. He knew the layout at Slash C headquarters. If he could get to the house unobserved and put a gun on Chastain, there'd be no need to make the Rimrocks roundup.

Deciding to give it a try, Troop swung off the cot. He was feeling for the lantern when the ploppity-plop of a galloping horse came plainly across the muddy yard, and now he heard Fern shout, 'Lew! Someone's coming.'

CHAPTER TEN

Joe Shedrow had spent most of the day delivering stove wood from the wagon yard behind Mitchell's Mercantile to various homes on Grand Avenue. It seemed, by grab, as if folks never wanted a stick of wood when the sun was shining; but let it come a shivery, rain-drenched day, and they all hollered for fuel. Raised Ned, too, because he couldn't supply 'em all at once. It was enough to sour a man's stomach.

Even Belle had put the hustle on him, wanting special short lengths for the little potbellied stove she'd set up in her room at the hotel. Joe hadn't minded that, though; he had stopped what he was doing and sawed her a supply right quick. When he toted it up to her room, there was Belle lying in bed pretty as you please having breakfast off a tray at ten o'clock in the morning.

'All that ruckus over Lew Troop kept me up half the night,' she told him. 'Have to get my beauty sleep.'

She sure looked like she had got it. Joe hadn't seen her more than once or twice since she'd left the dance hall. He looked at her now and said, 'You look elegant, Belle—just elegant.'

Belle smiled at him and set aside the tray. She yawned and stretched her arms up over her head. 'This is some different than it was when I lived with you, Joe. I guess you think I shouldn't of quit you like I did, but a girl can't go around with her feet sticking out of her shoes and not knowing where her next meal is coming from. I liked you fine, and still do— but I like having decent clothes and a soft bed to sleep in of a night.'

'Sure,' Joe said. When she told him to collect his pay for the wood down at the lobby desk, he came over to the bed and asked, 'How about a little kiss, just for old times' sake, Belle?'

She looked like maybe she would, and he leaned across the bed. But she pushed him back. 'It wouldn't be fitting, Joe—us being publicly separated and all.'

'I don't see what difference that makes,' Joe muttered, hugely disappointed. But he remembered that Belle had always been real strict in her morals. She had scarcely let him kiss her before they got preacher-married. And it looked, by grab, like she hadn't changed at all.

That suited Joe just fine. If she would continue being strict with her morals, they'd be back together one of these days. All that flirting and fussing with other men at the Bon Ton hadn't meant a thing, he decided. Belle wouldn't do anything really wrong. She might fun with the customers and act a trifle chancy, but there was nothing bad about her. Joe felt good, better than he'd felt in months. Just being near Belle for a few minutes, smelling that cold cream she had on her face and seeing her fancy lace drawers on a chair, had made him feel ten years younger. He hadn't minded toting wood all day in the rain and listening to gabby housewives jaw about him being late with deliveries. Belle, by grab, was still his woman!

Now, eating supper at the Chink's Café, Joe stuck a hand in his pants pocket and fondled the silk wad there. Belle's drawers smelled just like her. He smiled, thinking how she must have fretted when she couldn't find them.

It had been a big day for him, in more ways than one. He'd made upwards of ten dollars clear profit, and would probably make as much more tomorrow. Old Angus Mitchell supplied him with a horse and wagon, an ax, a bucksaw, and a place to sleep in the barn. They split fifty-fifty on the wood, Joe cutting it out on the Free Strip and hauling it to the Mercantile wagon yard for storage until folks ordered fuel. It wasn't what you'd call an easy-money proposition, but it gave a man some chance to treasure-hunt and eat at the same time.

Those were the two things Joe wanted to do most—eat and treasure-hunt. He finished his coffee and filled an ancient brier pipe and took his ease. The rush on wood deliveries should slack off in a day or so, then he'd drive out to Cemetery Slope and do some digging. He smiled, and felt the warming glow that always came when he thought about finding Curly Bill's cache. Belle had poked fun at him about it, calling it a pipe dream. Folks said he was treasure-loco, and Dade Chastain had ordered him to refill all the holes he dug so's no Slash C cows would fall into them. But the fun-pokers didn't know about the *derrotero* a drunken Mexican had sold him for five dollars—the map that showed almost exactly where the fabulous treasure was buried.

They'd sing another tune one of these days, by grab!

Especially Belle. He could imagine how her eyes would shine when she saw him drive into town with a wagon-load of gold and silver ornaments from that Mex mission in Matamoras. 'Why, Joe!' she'd exclaim. 'You found it—just like you promised me!'

And then she would call him 'honey,' like when they were first married.

111

Joe sighed, thinking how purely elegant everything would be when he found the cache. They would take a honeymoon trip, a real one this time, with no need to scrimp on money. They would sleep in the same bed again and things would be as they'd been when he and Belle were first married. It made him blush to think of it.

He had to find that hidden treasure! He just *had* to . . .

Sheriff Eggleston came into the café and ordered a cup of coffee. 'Make it hot and black,' he told Lon Sing. 'I got a cold ride in front of me.'

'You get word of Lew Troop's whereabouts?' Ike Ledbetter asked.

'No. I promised Dade I'd help with his Rimrocks gather, him bein' so short-handed. Didn't know the weather would be like this, though.'

'Did the Borgstrom woman show up yet?' Ledbetter asked.

'Haven't seen a sign of her,' Eggleston muttered, and rubbed his big, cold-reddened nose. 'I can't understand it, Ike. Dade must've run her off, like he planned. But nobody has seen hide or hair of her.'

Joe Shedrow had been so busy all day that he'd scarcely thought about last night's wild happenings. But now he wondered about Lew

Troop—if the tough drifter had kept Chastain from driving Miss Borgstrom off her homestead. That would be something, by grab! If Troop had done that all by himself, there'd be a chance for others to settle on the Free Strip. Him, even. He could do a heap of treasure-hunting if he had a shack out there on the Strip.

'Suppose I'd better stop by Swede's place on my way to Slash C and find out if she's still there,' the sheriff said.

Joe didn't like that idea. He put away his pipe and said meekly, 'Don't seem as if she would be, does it, Sheriff Bill? Not after what Mr. Chastain told her.'

'No, it don't. But it don't seem reasonable that she hasn't showed up in town, neither.'

He finished his coffee and lit up a cigar and said, 'I'll soon find out for sure.'

Joe paid for his supper, so gripped by his thoughts that he forgot his change until Lon Sing called him back for it. What if Eggleston sneaked up on Swede's cabin and got the drop on Troop?

Or shot him through a window?

That would be about the way Big Bill would do it. The sheriff wouldn't take any chances after the way Troop had run right through the three of them last night. Eggleston would shoot first and talk afterward.

Joe hurried outside, muttering to himself, 'Troop should be warned.'

It was still raining. Felt as if it might turn to sleet before the night was over. It would be downright uncomfortable, riding to Swede's place. Especially without a saddle. But if Troop was there, he should be told that Eggleston was coming. A man who had the guts to do what Troop had done deserved a fair chance.

'I've got to do it,' Shedrow told himself.

It was a bouncing, bruising journey for a man who'd never done much riding. The old wagon mare was hard-gaited, unused to galloping, and a poor trotter. But Joe pushed her hard, fearful that Eggleston might overtake him unless he hurried. He took more punishment than he gave the flounder-footed mare. By the time she splashed across Canteen Creek, Joe wished he had taken time to hitch the wagon. He felt as if he were blistered all the way to the ankles when the lamplit windows of Swede's cabin finally came to view.

'Lordy, Lordy,' Joe groaned, but he kept beating on the mare and rode into the muddy yard at a gallop.

A sorrel-haired woman flung open the cabin door. She shouted something as Joe pulled up; and then, as he got painfully down, Lew

Troop rushed across the lamplit yard with a gun in his hand.

'It's me—Shedrow!' Joe yelled, seeing the wicked shine of the gun's barrel.

Troop lowered the gun. 'Who's chasing you?' he demanded.

'Nobody, but Sheriff Eggleston is on his way here,' Joe announced. 'I thought you ought to know about it.'

Troop cursed. 'How far back?' he asked.

'Depends on how fast he's riding,' Joe said, and noticed how Swede's daughter stood with both hands clasped high on her breasts as if she'd been frightened. 'Big Bill was in the café when I left town.'

'Then there's time enough,' Troop said. The tough scowl changed to a smile now and he said, 'I'm much obliged, Joe—again.' He turned to Fern, adding, 'This is Joe Shedrow, a real good friend of mine, Miss Borgstrom.'

'Then come inside, Mr. Shedrow,' she invited, 'and have a cup of coffee.'

'Soon's I tie up the mare,' Joe agreed.

'I'll take her to the wagon shed,' Troop offered. 'Go in and dry yourself off.'

'What you goin' to do about Eggleston?' Joe asked. 'I wouldn't want him to find me here—unless you need my help.'

Troop chuckled. 'He won't find you,' Troop said, very confident about this. 'I'm

115

going out to meet the sheriff. You'll see no more of him tonight.'

Big Bill Eggleston was disgusted. Bad enough, he thought, to be at Dade Chastain's beck and call on sheriff-office matters without having to turn cowboy for him. He had told Dade as much, in a nice way, explaining that he wasn't a young buck any more. But Dade had turned those bleached-blue eyes on him and said, 'Neither am I. You be at the ranch tomorrow night, and bring your spurs. You'll need them.'

So here he was, saddle-polishing his pants with rain pelting his slicker. What a way for a man to spend the evening, especially a businessman who owned a fine hotel! He should be at the Palacial now, sweet-talking Belle Smith into letting him visit her room along about midnight with a bottle of Colonel's Monogram. If he could just get her drunk, she might forget her uppity ideas about being true to her no-account husband.

When Big Bill crossed Canteen Creek and came to the Free Strip turnoff, he pulled to a stop. Should he go by Swede's place, or ride straight on to Slash C? It meant upwards of five miles' extra riding in the rain. And the night was blacker'n the inside of a cow. Seemed unlikely that the Borgstrom woman was there. Chastain had said she'd be off the

116

place by noon, hadn't he? That meant she was off it.

But where had she gone?

Nobody had seen her drive through town. Nor had Lew Troop been seen. It sure beat all how he had disappeared last night. The black-haired bastard must have Indian blood in him. The thought came to Eggleston now that Troop might have gone out to Swede's place like he'd bragged. He might have put the run on Chastain's nester-removal committee. It didn't seem likely that one man could do such a thing; not even a tough one like Troop.

'But I'd better take a look, just for sure,' Big Bill muttered.

He turned into the north fork and had gone a dozen paces when his horse shied away from an obscure shape that loomed up in the trail. Then Lew Troop asked, 'Is that you, Bill?'

'Yes,' Eggleston said, too surprised and confused for evasion or thought of cautious concealment. 'What you doin' out here in the rain?'

'Waiting for you,' Troop said calmly. 'I'm riding out to Slash C with you.'

'To Slash C!' Eggleston blurted. 'How come you'd be goin' there?'

Troop chuckled. 'It's a long story,' he said, 'and one you should hear from Dade Chastain, who'll enjoy telling it. Especially the deal he

117

made with me to ride roundup for him.'

'You mean you're—'

'Yes,' Troop interrupted. 'Let's get going.'

Wholly bewildered, Eggleston turned and was into the Slash C road with Troop when he remembered about Swede's place. 'I got to find out if that Borgstrom woman is still there,' he announced.

'Didn't she come to town this morning?' Troop demanded.

'No, which makes me figger she never left.'

'She left, all right,' Troop reported. 'She was gone when I got there. That's how Dade and I happened to make our deal.'

Eggleston considered that in silence for a moment. 'Then she must've circled around Signal, or used a back street,' he decided.

'Shouldn't wonder,' Troop agreed, keeping his voice casual. 'Reckon she didn't want folks to poke fun at her.'

They were riding knee to knee when Troop rammed the muzzle of his gun against Eggleston's side and ordered roughly, 'Pull up—and do like I tell you.'

'What the hell!' Eggleston blurted.

'I should let you have it right now,' Troop muttered, prodding Eggleston so hard that the big lawman grunted. 'I should give it to you right through the gut.'

Eggleston sat perfectly still. For a moment

118

there was only the patter of rain on cold-stiffened slickers. Then Troop said, 'That was a damned raw deal last night. Three of you ganging up on me.'

'But I never fired at you,' Big Bill protested. 'I shot a few times, but not at you.'

'A liar by the clock,' Troop scoffed.

'That's the God's truth, Lew—the God's truth. I'd swear to it on a stack of Bibles. I was just puttin' on a show for Dade, is all. You know how it is. A sheriff has to go along with Chastain, even when he'd rather not. Him and Lee Monroe wanted you arrested, or shot in the attempt. But I figgered you'd high-tail out of town if you had the chance.'

Troop didn't say anything. He just waited, wanting Big Bill to keep talking.

'I was glad you made it,' Eggleton assured him. 'Hell, I never had nothin' agin you, Lew. Not a thing.' Then he asked soothingly, 'Why don't you ride south like you planned?'

'Because Chastain has my horse,' Troop said, 'and I'm not leaving without him.'

'But you got a horse,' Eggleston insisted. 'It ain't like you was afoot.'

'I wouldn't trade Blue for three jugheads like this one,' Troop said. 'That grulla is the best horse I ever rode.'

There was another interval of silence during which Sheriff Eggleston kept his hands on the

119

saddle horn. Then, in the eager way of a man wanting to make a trade, he offered, 'I'll get the grulla back for you, Lew. I'll go talk to Dade right now.'

'Sure,' Troop said. 'Sure you will.' Keeping the Walker's muzzle hard against Eggleston, he ordered, 'Reach in and unbuckle that gun belt with your left hand.' When the gun-weighted gear slid to the ground, Troop said, 'Now give me your law bracelets.'

'What for?' Big Bill demanded. 'You don't need to handcuff me.'

Troop rammed the gun hard against his ribs and Eggleston yelped, 'All right! All right!'

During the next five minutes Troop gave more orders, which Big Bill obeyed without further protest. When they rode on up the puddled trail, Eggleston was holding his reins with manacled hands, and his arms were secured behind his back by the loop of a rope that was fastened to Troop's saddle horn.

'What you got me trussed up like this for?' Eggleston asked indignantly.

'You'll find out when we reach Slash C,' Troop muttered, and wondered if his wild scheme would work. There was no way of knowing how a man like Chastain would react.

For a time they rode in silence, their horses splashing through mud that was fetlock-deep.

Chastain, Troop reasoned, would be expecting Big Bill, so there should be no trouble riding into the ranch yard unchallenged. After that, of course, it would depend on how Chastain responded to pressure. Dade, he supposed, had no real liking for this flabby-faced sheriff and ordinarily wouldn't much care what happened to him. But Dade was short-handed and needed every rider he could get. That might make a difference.

When lamplit windows showed in the rain-drizzled gloom directly ahead, Eggleston asked worriedly, 'Supposin' Dade won't give up the grulla?'

'Then he'll be short two roundup riders, instead of one,' Troop said flatly.

Eggleston cursed. 'You got that rope tied to your saddle horn?' he asked. And when Troop grunted assent, Big Bill whined, 'If they shoot you out of the saddle I'll get drug to death.'

'Yes,' Troop agreed. 'You sure as hell will.'

CHAPTER ELEVEN

Shortly after nine o'clock Dade Chastain stood in the bunkhouse doorway and said, 'You boys better wind up your poker playing. We'll

121

be asaddle at daylight.'

'You still think Troop will show up?' Oak Creek Kirby asked.

'I'm positive,' Chastain said.

'Ain't Eggleston supposed to ride with us tomorrow?' Monk Monroe inquired.

'He'll be here,' Chastain announced confidently.

Joe Maffitt snickered. 'Be the first day's work that starpacker has done in years. It should be somethin' to watch.'

'You'll have no time for gawking,' Chastain warned. 'I want those cattle worked fast—faster than you ever worked before. One day might mean the difference between getting 'em down or losing a big bunch.'

He crossed the yard then, observing that the rain had lessened to a misty drizzle. There was scarcely any wind now and the air seemed warmer. If the snows held off for one week there'd be sufficient time to gather every head of stock from the Rimrocks. That's what he wanted; every last head. The way the market was now, a man couldn't afford to lose stock.

Chastain stepped up to the kitchen stoop and scraped mud from his boots. He was reaching for the doorknob when he glimpsed a slickered shape approaching the house and heard Sheriff Eggleston call, 'Dade, it's me—Big Bill!'

Chastain peered at him and demanded, 'What you doing afoot?'

Eggleston had been walking, but now he stopped in the abrupt fashion of a roped steer. He teetered back on his heels as if yanked. 'I've got to git Lew Troop's horse,' he shouted.

'You drunk?' Chastain asked, wholly puzzled. 'Why you standing there like a loco sheepherder?'

Big Bill stood just inside the long shaft of lamplight from the kitchen window so that when he held up his manacled wrists the wet handcuffs made a metallic glint. 'I got to git that grulla—or be drug to death!'

That didn't make sense to Chastain. 'What in hell you talking about?' he demanded.

'I'm roped from behind,' Eggleston explained, his voice high-pitched with apprehension. 'Lew Troop has me snubbed to his saddle horn!'

Chastain probed the gloom and glimpsed a rain-blurred, barely visible shape some thirty or forty feet beyond Eggleston. Yet even now, with the realization of what Lew Troop had done rifling through him, Chastain could scarcely believe it. That Texas drifter must be haywire in the head. No man in his right mind would attempt such a damn-fool stunt. Not here, smack-dab in the yard. Troop must

123

think himself bulletproof.

'Have somebody bring out the grulla,' Eggleston called. 'This ain't no time to fuss, Dade. Can't you see the fix I'm in?'

The crew stood in the bunkhouse doorway, and now Monk Monroe asked, 'What's he talking about, boss?'

Chastain motioned for Monroe to come over to the scoop. If those lunkheads weren't so stupid they'd know enough to buckle on their guns and spread out to where they could shoot at Troop without hitting Eggleston. But they had to be told.

Monroe hadn't taken more than a step or two when Troop fired, the muzzle flare of his gun briefly revealing him asaddle with Eggleston's horse held close. Monk dodged back to the doorway, yelling, 'Put out that goddamn lamp and hand me a Winchester!'

'Don't do no shootin'!' Eggleston shouted. 'You'll git me killed!'

Chastain backed into the kitchen doorway. And now, as the bunkhouse went dark, Eggleston screamed, 'Dade! For God's sake, don't do no shootin'!'

The cook came padding in from his room behind the kitchen and yawned. 'What's all the commotion?'

'Put out the lamp,' Chastain ordered. Then he changed his mind. 'No, leave it on, so we

124

can see Eggleston.'

If those fools in the bunkhouse would just slip out now and come around Troop, they'd have him boxed without risk to Big Bill. Surely they'd know enough for that. Even a lunkheaded cowpuncher would have that much sense. Chastain watched for sign of movement near the bunkhouse; listened for the sound of stealthy walking.

'What you waitin' on, Dade?' Eggleston called anxiously. 'Bring out Troop's horse, for God's sake!'

Chastain ignored that plea, expectantly waiting for guns to blast out in the yard. He peered into the misty gloom, hoping to see movement. He said to the cook, 'Get my gun from the office.'

If they got behind Troop he'd have to ride this way.

'You want me to try a shot?' Monk Monroe called from the bunkhouse. 'I got a Winchester.'

Chastain cursed. The witless fools hadn't taken a step. They were still in the bunkhouse, waiting to be told. And he couldn't tell them what to do without Troop's hearing.

'One of you bring me the grulla,' Eggleston pleaded. 'Dade, I won't be no use to you on roundup if I'm drug to death. Can't you see that?' And when Chastain remained silent, Big Bill urged, 'You're short-handed already, ain't you? If a rumpus starts now, somebody besides me might get hurt, and then where's your roundup? All you got to do is give Troop back his horse and he'll ride right out of the country.'

Chastain shrugged. Big Bill, he supposed, was right. No sense risking the loss of a whole herd just to spite one shiftless saddle bum. But it went against the grain; by God, it went against the grain something awful!

'All right, I'll do it your way,' Chastain said sharply. 'And you'll do two men's work to make up for Troop. You'll ride like you never rode before!'

Then he called, 'Monk, bring out that goddamn grulla!'

Lew Troop was three miles east of Slash C when he gave Blue a breather. Halting in the dark road, he listened for sound of pursuit, and hearing none, announced, 'We're shut of them, kid.'

He wiped his wet hands on his shirt and built a cigarette and thought how lucky he'd been. They'd had him four to one, not counting the cook, and he hadn't spoken a word until Big Bill walked up to him with Blue. Troop chuckled, recalling how he had praised Eggleston while transferring his

126

saddle to the grulla, telling Big Bill what a good sheriff he'd turned out to be; and how sourly Eggleston had thanked him for the thonged key to the handcuffs.

That was one time Big Bill Eggleston had done his duty, by God. He had recovered a stolen horse.   —

There had been a bad moment or two as he'd ridden off. Dade Chastain had shouted for Eggleston to get down, and someone at the bunkhouse—Monroe,   most   likely—had opened up with a Winchester. But he had made no target at all, and none of those random shots had come close to him.

Riding on toward the road fork, Troop felt a high sense of satisfaction in what had been accomplished. Dade Chastain had used fear as a weapon to have his way in Cathedral Basin on countless occasions; fear had been his chief stock in trade. But tonight it had worked the other way. Big Bill Eggleston's fear of being dragged to death had beaten Chastain.

'In his own dooryard,' Troop reflected and recalling how eager Monk Monroe had been to use a Winchester, he muttered, 'Two can play the shooting game.'

It would come to that eventually, he understood. They wouldn't use their fists on him again. They'd use guns.

When he came to the Free Strip turnoff

Troop dismounted. Thumbing a match aflame, he scanned the hoof-pocked mud and observed the fresh tracks of Joe Shedrow's big-footed mare headed toward town. That meant Fern was alone at the cabin. Troop grinned and got back into the saddle. Fern had acted downright worried when he left. She had been afraid for him, and showed it in the way she said, 'Be careful, Lew. Please be careful.'

It occurred to Troop now that he might have tallied her wrong, thinking she would settle for nothing less than marriage. Perhaps if she really liked a man . . .

You just couldn't tell about women. They said one thing, and meant another.

Troop urged Blue to a faster pace. He hummed a verse of 'Hell among the Yearlings' and wondered if Fern would be waiting up for him.

She was. She stood in the cabin doorway and called, 'Is it you?' in an eager, wishful voice. Then, as he rode into the doorway's shaft of lamplight, she exclaimed, 'You got your horse!'

She made a lovely picture standing there with the lamp's soft glow behind her. She was like the flame-forged vision a lonely man sometimes saw in his campfire—the warmth and the fragrance a man dreamed of finding,

128

and seldom found.

She asked, 'Would you like a cup of coffee, Lew?'

Troop nodded, not aware that he was gawking at her until she asked, 'Is there something odd about me?'

'Not odd,' Troop said.

He cuffed back the brim of his rain-sogged hat and grinned at her. 'Just the best-looking boss a hired man ever had.'

Fern smiled acknowledgment of that compliment. She asked, 'Are you Irish?'

'About half. Why?'

'That explains the blarney talk,' she said, and turned back into the cabin. 'I'll put on the coffeepot.'

Troop whistled a cheery tune as he led Blue into the open end of the wagon shed. Fetching the lantern from his bunk room, he unsaddled and gave Blue a double ration of grain from the supply Fern had brought in the wagon.

'We're eating high off the hog, you and me,' he told the gelding. 'A midnight snack for both of us.'

Going back across the yard, Troop wondered if Chastain might have sent riders to trail him toward town, guessing that he would put up in Signal for the night. If he had, the search might end up here. He listened for a moment, hearing no sound save the steady dripping of rain water off the eaves, and when he stepped into the cabin all thought of trouble was banished by the fine smell of boiling coffee and fresh-baked apple pie. Peering at the generous wedge of pie Fern had placed on the table for him, Troop smacked his lips and asked, 'Do you always bake at night?'

'No,' she said, pouring his coffee. 'But I needed to be busy. It's hard to just sit and wait, and worry.'

Troop hung his hat and slicker on the wall peg. He asked, 'Worried about me, ma'am?'

She nodded. 'You might have been shot.'

'Not with the old dame's arm around me.'

'What old dame?'

'Dame Fortune.'

Fern laughed at him. 'I've always heard the Irish were superstitious,' she said.

The way she said it, sort of teasing, and the way she looked, did something to Lew Troop.

'Did you hear the Irish are romantic also?' he asked, and stepped around the table toward her.

Fern didn't answer. And she didn't back away from him. The smile faded from her cheeks and she looked now as she had that day at Canteen Creek when he'd offered to muck out the cabin. There was the same upchinned tilt to her face, the same expression in her eyes.

'Don't you like apple pie?' she asked without excitement.

That stopped him. It reminded him of what Monk Monroe had said about her being cold. By God, she looked cold now. Cold as ice.

'I thought all men liked apple pie,' Fern said calmly.

'Sure,' Troop muttered, resenting her composure and endeavoring to match it. 'Men like other things too.'

Her blue eyes met his unflinchingly with self-confidence and a serenity that baffled Lew Troop. She knew what he wanted. Any woman would know that. But it didn't ruffle her at all. Troop couldn't understand it.

'Drink your coffee while it's hot,' Fern suggested.

Coffee and apple pie. That's all she wanted to talk about at a time like this. Troop swore softly, dejectedly. Her acting worried had sure fooled him. It just went to show that you couldn't tell about women. He shrugged and walked around to his chair, loosing the self-mocking chuckle of a man laughing at himself.

'Is there a joke?' Fern inquired.

'Yes, and it's on me.'

He sat down and sampled the coffee before adding, 'I thought you were worried about

131

Lew Troop. But it was a hired man. You'd have fretted just as much if his name was Bill Smith. Hired men are hard to come by on the Free Strip. You didn't want yours killed, or crippled so he couldn't haul firewood.'

'So?' Fern murmured.

'So you get what you hired—a man to do the chores for one month, after which time he'll high-tail south like hell wouldn't have him.'

Fern nodded agreement. She said, 'Joe Shedrow told me that if I stay here for one month there'll be four or five settlers who'll return to their homesteads. Think what a change one month may bring.'

'Joe's head is full of wishful notions,' Troop muttered. 'He's dug half a hundred holes on Cemetery Slope, trying to find buried treasure that might've been hidden fifty miles away, or dug up by someone else, or never really buried. You can't put much store in what a man like that tells you.'

The half-smiling expression altered Fern's cheeks. 'But Joe Shedrow has his dream of finding the treasure,' she said softly. 'It's good for a man to have something big to work for—something to give him hope. That's the best part of it, the hope. Mr. Shedrow told me about his wife. He's very much in love with her. That's why he's digging for hidden

132

treasure, so that he can buy things for his wife. The nice things she never had.' Then she asked, 'Do you know her?'

Troop nodded, and recalling what Belle had said about this sorrel-haired woman, he felt a disturbing sense of guilt. Belle had said Swede's daughter wouldn't give him anything. She'd been right about that, but not the rest of it. Looking at Fern now, Troop marveled at Belle's jealous slander. Uppity, Belle had called her. But she wasn't uppity at all. She was kind and gentle. And she was made the way a woman should be.

That was the hell of it. She had everything a man wanted in a woman. But she didn't want a man . . .

Troop shrugged and asked, 'Aren't you having coffee?'

'It would keep me awake, so late at night,' she explained.

Presently, when Troop had finished his pie, he asked, 'What do you want done tomorrow?' adding with mock politeness, 'Boss, ma'am.'

'My father brought a Jersey heifer with him from Texas,' she said. 'If you can find it I'll keep it penned so we can have milk and butter.'

'Is a hired man supposed to do the milking?' Troop demanded.

133

Fern smiled and said, 'I'll do it.'

As he reached for his hat and slicker, she asked, 'Wouldn't it be well to bring in the cows with calves so that they can be fed hay when the snow comes?'

'Yes,' Troop agreed. 'Probably aren't more than five or six, counting the Jersey.'

'Then bring them in,' she said, and was clearing off the table when he went out.

Afterward, lying on his cot in the bunk room, Troop reviewed the night's curious happenings and took no satisfaction in them. Fern Borgstrom wouldn't change. Come hell or high water, he'd never be more than a hired man to her. She was what Big Bill Eggleston had called her: mule-stubborn.

'One month of this will be aplenty,' he muttered.

CHAPTER TWELVE

In four days of steady riding Lew Troop brought five cows with calves to the tree-bordered meadow south of the Borgstrom cabin. He circled so far west that he observed Slash C riders working cattle on the lower ridges; he talked with Joe Shedrow, who was digging a new treasure hole on Cemetery

Slope; he scouted all the hills, and the valleys that lay between them. But he didn't find the Jersey heifer.

'Must've died,' Troop told Fern at supper on the fourth evening. 'Jerseys don't do good on the open range.'

'Have you searched all the places she might be?' Fern asked.

'All the places she ought to be,' Troop said gruffly. 'The heifer might've crossed Canteen Creek, but it doesn't seem likely. There isn't enough grass on the east side to feed a goat.'

'Then look there tomorrow,' Fern suggested. 'We mustn't let her starve.'

'I should be hauling firewood instead of looking for a cow that the coyotes probably got six months ago,' Troop objected.

But Fern said, 'One more day's search might find her.'

Troop grimaced. All this searching for one measly milk cow. You'd have thought the heifer was Fern's kinfolk the way she worried about it.

'I'll take a look east of Canteen Creek after I get in some firewood,' Troop said. 'We're almost out, and this is no time to be caught short of fuel.'

Presently, while Troop smoked his after-supper cigarette, Fern explained why she was so set on finding the heifer. 'My father thought more of the Jersey than all his other cows put together. She was a sort of symbol. Do you understand what I mean, Lew?'

'You mean she's homesteader stock, whereas the others are cow-ranch beef critters?'

Fern nodded smilingly, pleased that he understood. 'It took faith to bring a Jersey here. The faith of a man who intended to farm his land—who intended to grow something besides a calf crop. That's why I want you to find her, Lew. My father is dead, but the dream he had is not dead. And the Jersey heifer is part of that dream.'

'But I haul some firewood first,' Troop said, 'or the dream might turn into a nightmare.'

When he opened the door to leave he teetered back on his heels as if struck. 'Look,' he said, pulling the door back so that she could see. 'It's snowing right now!'

The snow turned to rain during the night. There was only a thin drizzle when Troop harnessed the team after breakfast, and it petered out entirely by the time he drove across the yard.

Fern stood in the doorway, watching. She called, 'The sun may be shining soon,' and waved to him.

Sun, hell, Troop thought. More likely to

136

snow again.

★   ★   ★

For five days then, while huge cloud banks formed an ominous barricade all across Cathedral Basin's north rim, Lew Troop toiled with team and ax from dawn till dark. Choosing a timbered ridge just west of Canteen Creek where windfalls were plentiful, he had set himself the stint of trimming out and cutting a load of wood by noon so that it could be hauled home before sundown.

It took some doing.

The first morning had been hell. Blisters formed on the palms of his hands; his arms, unaccustomed to such tedious work, had ached with each swing of the double-bitted ax. By noon, when he began loading the logs, Troop was exhausted. This, he decided, was no fit chore for a riding man, and was tempted to quit—to tell Fern Borgstrom she'd have to hire somebody else. But at dusk he had driven into the yard with a load of seasoned logs and found Fern waiting in the lamplit doorway.

'Any trouble?' she asked.

'Trouble enough,' he'd told her, dog-tired and grouchy. 'Swinging an ax is the worst trouble a man could have.'

She helped him unhitch the team. But

except for needful talk, she didn't say much that evening, or the next day, or the day after that. Until last night at supper, when she announced, 'Tomorrow is Sunday, Lew. Take a day of rest.'

And when he shrugged off that suggestion, she had said, 'You're losing weight. That's not good for so thin a man.'

That had surprised Troop and pleased him. He hadn't thought she gave a damn if he worked himself to a shrunk-up nubbin. It was no meat off her rump what happened to a knot-headed hired man, just so she got a full day's work for a day's wages. It had pleasured him to find out different. But he didn't follow her suggestion to take Sunday off.

There was a blizzard building in the mountains. Every sign pointed to it. This windless, sunless weather was the calm before a big storm. The cattle knew it. The five cows and their calves had come to the corral fence yesterday, hunting shelter. Even Blue, who'd never been in a blizzard, seemed to know what was coming, for he stayed close to the wagon-shed of the horse trap.

They would need plenty of firewood on hand—fuel enough to keep the stove going day and night. No telling how long the blizzard would last. Might be only a day or two; but it could last for a week, and they'd be snowed in for a month afterward.

'I was just a slick-eared boy in the winter of the Big Die in Texas,' Troop told Fern, 'but I'll never forget it.'

He shivered, remembering how whole families had perished on the snow-piled Panhandle because they'd run short of fuel. That winter of his boyhood had marked him; it made him fret about firewood.

Although Troop didn't mention it, another thing was fretting him. The Slash C roundup would be finished now, which meant that Chastain might soon learn that he had neighbors. Unwelcome neighbors. One man couldn't stand them off forever. Not if they kept trying. Troop wondered how soon Chastain would discover that Swede's cabin was occupied. Might be today—or not for a week. That would be the worst part of it—the waiting and the wondering. The not knowing. It would fret a man more with each day's passing so that he'd start wearing his gun at the supper table.

Now, as Troop finished eating his supper, Fern asked, 'Are you worried about the storm that's brewing?'

Two storms, Troop thought. But he said, 'No use to worry.'

As was his custom, Troop sat in the rocker beside the stove for a leisurely cigarette before going to his room in the wagon shed. And because Fern invariably busied herself clearing off the table, he had his brief interval of replenishing the picture she had made for him that first evening. Even though he understood that she wasn't for him, he liked to watch the graceful movements of her body as she walked from table to sink. She would make some man a fine wife. But he'd have to be the right kind; a hard-working homesteader who'd be willing to fight for his land. A sober, stubborn, strong-backed man who would pick up a handful of dirt and watch it sift from his calloused palm and say, 'It is good.'

Troop wondered if she would be more free-talking with her husband; if she would allow him to remain in this room of a Saturday night while she took her tub bath. She had a composure and a reserve that challenged a man's imagination, that made him speculate on the chance of breaking through her shield of aloofness. Was she as content and self-sufficient as she seemed, or did she have the hungers a modest woman kept concealed?

There had been a time or two when Troop was tempted to find out—when the thrusting urge to take her in his arms had been almost more than he could resist. But on these occasions he remembered how it had been the night she asked, 'Don't you like apple pie?'

And there was in him also an instinctive wariness against a future filled with homesteader toil. A man could get himself trapped with a woman like Fern Borgstrom; might barter his freedom for the privilege of learning about her hidden hungers. She wouldn't reveal them without a wedding ring, or leave this place that was a monument to the memory of her father.

A man might better keep his hands in his pockets.

Troop flipped his cigarette butt into the stove grate and picked up his hat. He was at the door when Fern said, 'Take tomorrow off, Lew. Ride into town and have a drink, if that would please you.'

A self-mocking smile slanted Troop's gaunt face. 'That's for shiftless, scatter-heel cowpokes. Us woodchoppers are a different breed, ma'am. We don't waste time guzzling bar whisky or fussing with fancy women or playing poker. We just work and eat and sleep, day in and day out. We never celebrate, not even on Saturday nights. All we do is work, and collect our reward in heaven when we die.'

She showed him a queer, veiled glance, as if that rebellious attitude struck a responsive cord; as if these past few days of preparing meals that were eaten in silence might have plagued her. Troop thought he detected an expression of discontent in her eyes, but that wishful thought was banished when she said, 'That's not enough for a foot-loose man, is it, Lew?'

And then she said quietly, 'I'll not hold you to staying the full month, if you'd like to leave sooner. There should be firewood eough now, and I'll go look for the Jersey heifer myself.'

Troop shook his head. 'I'll stay the month. I'll spend tomorrow looking for the Jersey. Then I'll haul more stovewood and have it piled six feet high all across the back wall of this cabin when I leave.'

Fern smiled. She asked wonderingly, 'Then you'll ride off—just to be riding?'

'To get into the desert sun and let it thaw the cold out of me,' Troop corrected. A gust of wind whined past the cabin. He grimaced, saying, 'Hear that? It's old man winter blowing his cold breath ahead of him.'

Fern laughed, making an open-palmed gesture of resignation with her hands. 'Life is not perfect,' she mused. 'It's part winter and part summer, part joy and part sorrow. People change, sometimes. But life doesn't change. It's always part winter and part summer.'

Lew Troop thought about that as he entered his cheerless bunk room. A homesteader's life, he reflected, was mostly winter, meaning work, and damn little summer, meaning relaxation. It took all a man's energy to scratch out a bare living. Troop yawned wearily and sat on his cot and wondered where homestead men found the inclination or ambition to breed families. A man had to have a stallion streak in him to feel romantic after chopping wood all day.

Troop had one boot off and was tugging at the other when he heard a remote sound of hoofbeats. Instantly alert, he pulled the boot back on and listened. For a moment, as he got his gun from its peg on the wall, he thought his imagination must have tricked him. Then the sound came again, with a distinctness that was unmistakable—a rhythmic thudding in the night.

Almost at once then two hard-ridden horses ran through the yard. Their riders fired four shots, one of those slugs ricocheting off some metal part of the wagon, which stood in front of the shed. There was a shrill screech, strangely horrible above the drumming hoofbeats, and two more gunblasts ripped across the yard's quilted darkness.

Slash C riders, Troop thought. Monk Monroe and Oak Creek Kirby, most likely.

CHAPTER THIRTEEN

Troop ducked through the tarp-draped doorway in time to see an indistinct blur of motion over near the corral. He fired, and heard a man's voice lift in angry cursing, and ran to the wagon. One rider began circling the yard, yellow spurts of muzzle flame briefly indicating his course as he fired again and again. A bullet struck the wagon's seat, splintering its back board; another, caroming off a metal brace, made a twanging sound as it flew past Troop's head. That yonder son had his range.

Troop fired at him, and was aware of an urgent sense of pleasure. This was what he'd been dreading; but now that it was here he felt good about it. Only the waiting had been bad.

Observing that a shaft of lamplight lay across the muddy yard, Troop peered at the cabin and saw Fern standing in the doorway. 'Put out that lamp!' he called, moving swiftly along the wagon as bullets smashed into the sideboards.

But instead of extinguishing the light, Fern came out into the yard.

Astonished at such fantastic foolishness, Troop shouted, 'Go back! Go back!'

'No,' she called calmly. 'This is my dooryard and I walk where I please.'

Troop cursed. The woman must be daft.

'Get back before you get yourself shot!' he commanded.

But she paid him no heed. Peering across the yard, she called, 'Tell Mr. Chastain that his bluff didn't work.'

Bluff, hell! Those two weren't bluffing, and she'd soon find it out. What a fool she was! What a stupid, stubborn fool!

But no shot was fired while she crossed the yard. And now, as she came to stand directly in front of the wagon with her white blouse making a gray shadow against the darkness, there was a continuing silence.

'Are you all right, Lew?' she asked.

'Get around here behind the wagon,' he ordered.

'No need to,' Fern said calmly. 'They're leaving.'

Troop canted his head to listen, and heard horses moving off beyond the corral. He couldn't understand that the fight was over; couldn't believe that Fern's crazy notion to walk out here had ended it. He thought those riders would swing around for another run through the yard. But the diminishing hoof tromp told him that they were riding off.

'I knew they would stop shooting if I

145

walked out here,' Fern said.

'How could you know that?' Troop demanded.

'Well, I didn't know it, exactly,' she admitted. 'But I was quite sure.'

'How so?' Troop insisted. 'How could you be quite sure of a thing like that?'

'Come have a cup of coffee while I explain it,' Fern invited, taking his arm and walking close to him as they went across the yard.

Troop didn't like that. He pulled away and said stiffly, 'I don't want a woman to shield me.'

He holstered his gun, but he couldn't relax, couldn't quell the fighting tension that had filled him with a lust for conflict. And he couldn't understand why Monroe and Kirby had quit just because a woman pulled a damn-fool stunt. They had no respect for a homestead woman. They might not shoot at one deliberately, but they wouldn't quit firing just for fear of hitting her. Yet they had run off like a pair of spooked rabbits. It was beyond understanding.

Troop sat in the rocker and built a cigarette while Fern warmed up the coffee. He asked, 'What made you think they'd stop shooting if you came out?'

'It's quite simple,' she explained smilingly. 'Men are not mysterious. They are not difficult to read and understand. Some men are afraid of men and bold toward women. Others are afraid of women. Dade Chastain is.'

'Afraid?'

Fern nodded. 'I guessed it that first night when he came here with the sheriff. It showed in Mr. Chastain's eyes, and in the way he spoke to me. I watched him closely, seeing the nervous way his fingers kept opening and closing as he talked. I said to myself, This man is afraid of women, but I wasn't convinced until the next morning when he warned his men that they must not be rude to me. Then I was sure of it. Dade Chastain reminded me of my uncle in Texas. Uncle Jack was very rough with men and horses. A swearing, fighting terror. But he couldn't stand to see a woman mistreated. Any woman. It didn't matter if she was young or old, nice or trifling. Tears in the eyes of a dance-hall trollop would make him go to pieces.'

That explanation didn't satisfy Troop. 'All right, supposing Chastain is afraid of women. But it was Monroe and Kirby who were doing the shooting. Don't try to tell me they're afraid of women too, because I know better. Those two parlor-house sports rate a woman just one notch above a mare.'

'Perhaps so, Lew. But they're afraid of

disobeying Chastain. You notice they didn't once shoot toward the house. They were told to shoot you and were warned against hurting me.' A pleased, self-satisfied smile curved her lips now and she said, 'I guessed right, didn't I, Lew?'

'Seems so,' Troop admitted, marveling at the courage that had prompted her to back a conviction at such risk. Few women that he'd ever known would have done it. 'You might have guessed wrong, and got yourself shot.'

Fern shrugged. 'It was a chance I had to take,' she said, bringing him a cup of coffee. 'I was afraid you might get killed.'

She gave him a brief, slanting glance and turned back to the stove. But Troop glimpsed the color that stained her cheeks, saw the girlish confusion that momentarily displaced her queenly composure.

He knew then that Monk Monroe had been wrong about her. All wrong. She wasn't cold. She fairly glowed with womanly warmth. Troop couldn't take his eyes off her. It was as if a magnetic wave flowed between them—some impelling force so essential that it drew him to her at once.

'Fern!' he said huskily, reaching out to take her in his arms.

For an instant, as she stood there with the coffeepot tilted for pouring, a kindred eagerness warmed her eyes and the half-smiling expression altered her high-boned cheeks. She was at this moment more beautiful than he had supposed her to be, more radiant and more open to him that she'd ever been. More desirable.

But even as his hands grasped her shoulders Fern backed away, holding to the coffeepot and saying, 'No, Lew.' Not fearfully, nor excitedly, but with a plain dismissal that bewildered him. Now she said calmly, 'It wouldn't work out, Lew. You'd never be satisfied here, and I'd make a poor companion for a—a fiddle-footed man.'

Troop turned back to the table. He said, 'You think I'm just a saddle bum, don't you?'

'A drifter,' she said, not smiling. 'A man who runs away from winter—who wants summer the year round.'

'Is it wrong to want pleasant things like sunshine, or a warm-eyed woman?' Troop demanded.

And then, because anger and frustration were having their rough way with him, Troop strode out of the cabin, slamming the door behind him.

★   ★   ★

Dade Chastain was standing on the front

gallery when Monroe and Kirby rode into the Slash C yard. 'How'd it go?' he called.

'Not so good,' Monk reported.

They came on up to the house and dismounted. 'We shot at the wagon shed, like you told us,' Kirby explained. 'Troop came out and forted up behind a wagon. We'd of got him sure, just by circlin' back and forth, if the woman hadn't messed up the deal.'

'How could she mess it up?' Chastain demanded.

'You should of seen her,' Monk said. 'By God, she's the most loco female I ever saw, and I've seen some queer ones!'

'What did she do?' Chastain insisted.

Monk made a slapping motion with his head. 'Not a thing, boss—except come right across that goddamn yard and stand in front of Troop so's we had to quit shootin'. That's all she done. You'd of thought, by God, she knowed you told us not to shoot nowhere near her!'

'We should of put a couple of slugs past her bustle,' Kirby muttered. 'If ever a woman needed scarin', she does. She's brassy as a copper-bottomed kettle.'

'No, that wouldn't accomplish anything,' Chastain said.

He took a cigar from his pocket, bit off its end, and rolled it back and forth between his

150

lips for a moment before saying, 'You'll have to catch Troop away from the cabin.'

'But that might take a week,' Monroe objected. 'Why don't we all just ride in there and put the blast on that outfit, woman or no woman?'

Chastain lit the cigar, his face showing a deep-rutted scowl in the match flare. 'I want it done different,' he said. 'You're to catch Troop away from the cabin—the farther, the better. That means you're to be near Swede's place early tomorrow morning, and every morning, until you get that goddamn drifter.'

'I thought we was to have a few days off after roundup,' Monk complained.

'Not till Troop is taken care of,' Chastain said. 'Business comes first.'

CHAPTER FOURTEEN

It was raining when Troop rode out of the yard the next morning; a cold, wind-slanted rain turning to sleet. Fern, who had treated him with her habitual civility at breakfast, called to him as he passed the cabin, 'I do hope you find the Jersey.'

'Maybe I'll find her carcass, and bring you the hide,' Troop said grumpily.

Tilting his hat brim against the cold rain, he held Blue to a slow lope. The grulla was full of run this morning; he wanted to get up and go. But there was no telling how many miles of circling it would take to find that goddamn Jersey. He might never find her, but one thing he was sure of: If she was alive she must be somewhere east.

Troop was crossing Canteen Creek when Joe Shedrow drove his ancient wagon down the opposite bank. The wood peddler's cold-reddened face barely showed above the tarp that shrouded him from head to foot. He looked, Troop thought, like a mummy wrapped for burying.

'What you doing out so early on such a stinking day?' Troop greeted.

'Got a job of digging to do,' Joe said smilingly. 'I want to git it finished before the ground freezes too hard.'

'Any sign of treasure?'

Joe shook his head. 'But I'm sure it's there. According to the symbols on my map, it's got to be about where I'm diggin'. Just a case of findin' it, is all.'

Troop laughed at him. 'A trifling matter,' he suggested, not bothering to conceal his sarcasm. Any man who'd dig treasure holes on a day like this should have his head examined for screw worms. And Joe, according to what

Fern had said, was doing it for Belle Smith. What a joke that was!

'You ain't headin' for town, be you?' Shedrow asked. 'Sheriff Eggleston is back from roundup.'

'No,' Troop muttered, riding on. 'Us homesteaders seldom go to town. We can't take time from our chores.'

'Then what you doin' out here?'

'I'm hunting for a symbol,' Troop said disgustedly.

Shedrow wondered about that as he drove across the ford. Troop, he supposed, was joshing him about the map symbols. But why would he be riding east of Canteen Creek if he wasn't going to town?

Joe urged the mare to a faster pace. And because hope was high in him this day he said to her, 'You might have a heavy load to pull, goin' back to town.'

Just thinking about it made Joe feel warmer. Even though he was shivering, he felt warm inside. There were only one or two spots where that treasure could be; well, three or four at most. He had dug in all the other likely places, which meant he might strike the treasure cache today.

Joe smiled, thinking how wonderful that would be. Belle would forget all about their being separated. She'd be so shouting happy that she'd probably kiss him right in front of everybody. Joe felt of the silk wad in his pants pocket and chuckled, remembering how Belle had accused him of stealing her fancy drawers. A man should be entitled to that much to remember his wife by.

Shedrow was two miles along the road when Monk Monroe and Oak Creek Kirby came splashing up to the wagon.

'Did you meet Troop?' Monroe asked.

Joe shook his head.

'You sure about that?' Kirby demanded.

Joe shivered, so cold now that he could scarcely keep his teeth from chattering. These two Slash C toughs looked even more ornery than usual.

Monk Monroe spurred his horse close to the wagon. 'Didn't you see Troop back there a ways?'

'No,' Joe said.

'Why, you goddamn lyin' nester!' Monk bellowed and slashed at Shedrow with the barrel of his revolver.

Joe tried to duck, but the barrel caught him on the left temple. It knocked him back so that he fell into the wagon bed and lay with his tarp-wrapped shoulders across the handles of a pick and shovel.

'I'll learn you to lie to your betters,' Monk snarled, and now, as Joe dazedly propped himself up, Monk hit him again.

'That fixed him,' Kirby said, seeing how Shedrow lay. 'Now let's go fix that goddamn Troop.'

They rode on then, and the mare, wanting to follow them toward town, began turning the wagon. A front wheel cramped against the wagon box. Roused by that scraping racket and the sleety rain pelting his face, Joe Shedrow sat up. There was a pounding ache across his temples and his eyes didn't seem to focus properly. He peered about, identifying his location, but not remembering how he'd got there. Everything seemed odd to him, as if he were dreaming. He wondered why the mare had tried to turn around, and why he'd been lying down.

'Must've fell asleep,' Joe muttered.

Picking up the lines, he swung the mare back into the road's hoof-pocked mud.

All the way to Cemetery Slope, Joe wondered why he had fallen asleep. Must be the cold, he decided, observing how the mare's breath jetted out in smoke-like puffs. But why was his head aching so? And what was the matter with his eyes?

When the mare stopped at the hole he'd started digging yesterday, Joe unwound the tarp and got down. He slipped on the sleety ground and saved himself by grasping a wheel. If anyone saw him now they'd guess he'd been drinking, Joe thought. That's how he felt—half drunk.

There was a coating of ice on the shovel handle. When he began digging the ice melted and wet his mittens. Each shovelful of rain-sogged earth seemed heavier than the one that preceded it. God-awful heavy. But the digging warmed him so that his teeth stopped chattering. By the time he had the hole hip-deep he was sweating.

Joe rested, and dug again, and rested. This hole, he decided, should be dug differently from the others. The ground might be frozen hard tomorrow. Instead of separate holes, he'd dig a circular trench and cover more territory.

The rain ceased sometime during the morning. Later a cold wind swept down the slope, chilling Joe to the bone each time he stopped to rest. But thought of the treasure warmed him. There'd be gold candlesticks big around as a man's wrist in Curly Bill's cache; golden images and all sorts of fabulous trinkets from that Mex mission. He would be the wealthiest man in Arizona Territory when he found them.

Joe's shovel clanged against a boulder. He dug around it, got it loose, and made three unsuccessful attempts before finally lifting it out. The trench was shoulder-high at this end—almost deep enough. He dug again and struck what he thought was another boulder. But when he scraped the dirt away he saw metal—the rusted corner of what looked like a trunk. For a moment he just stared at it. Then he went to his knees, clawed more dirt away, and glimpsed wood and flat bands of iron.

'A treasure chest!' he croaked.

Digging frantically now, he observed its huge size and the massive padlock.

This was it—the treasure he'd been seeking so long. Curly Bill's cache!

He laughed and cried and pounded on the big trunk with his mittened hands. Wait till Belle heard about this!

It occurred to him now that he couldn't possibly lift the trunk out by himself. He'd have to get help. But who? Who could he trust?

'Lew Troop,' Joe told himself. Lew was his good friend. The tough Texan would help him.

In a frenzy of haste Joe climbed out of the trench and started for the wagon. Then he ran back to the trench. It wouldn't do to leave the treasure chest uncovered. Some Slash C rider might ride past and see it, and claim it for his own. So thinking, Joe got back into the hole and quickly covered the trunk top with dirt.

Then, panting and so weak he staggered, Joe hurried to the wagon.

It wasn't far to Swede Borgstrom's place. Lew Troop would gladly help him.

And wouldn't Belle be tickled? She'd be proud to be his wife now, by grab—purely proud!

Joe slapped the mare with the lines. 'Git a hustle on you,' he commanded, shouting against the wind. 'I've found Curly Bill's cache!'

The wind was bitter cold against Joe's sweat-soaked body, and he'd left the tarp back there on the ground. But he was warm inside. Folks wouldn't be poking fun at him any more. And Belle wouldn't be working at the Palacial this time tomorrow. She'd be with him, on a stage headed for Tucson.

A treasure chest!

CHAPTER FIFTEEN

There wasn't a sign of the Jersey heifer as Troop rode wide circles northward, scanning the ground for fresh tracks. Except for one slat-ribbed old bull, he didn't see a cow critter all morning. A damn-fool errand, this, he thought disgustedly. But what could a man

158

expect when he hired out to a woman—a mule-stubborn woman?

Troop wondered how soon there'd be another night raid on the wagon shed. Soon, he supposed, for Dade Chastain wasn't a man to bide his time where the Free Strip was concerned. It seemed odd that Dade should be so strict about not hurting a woman. In all the time he had known him, Chastain had never once shown the slightest interest in women; had seemed contemptuous of them, in fact. Yet Fern had recognized Dade's secret weakness and was using it against him.

It occurred to Troop now that she was also using another man's weakness—his own Texas pride. Fern Borgstrom was a smart woman. Too damn smart.

Shortly after noon Troop turned south, working the same territory over, but keeping to the ridges. Where was that stinking Jersey heifer? Or her carcass. If he could just find out for sure that she had died there'd be an end of it. A dead symbol.

It was bitter cold on these elevations. Troop's stiff slicker turned the wind, but there was no warmth to it, and not much more to the leather jacket he wore. A man should have a fleeced-lined short coat for winter riding, and woolen mittens. Troop considered the idea of going into Signal and outfitting

159

himself right now. It wasn't far to town, and Big Bill Eggleston wouldn't give him any trouble. The sheriff might want to, but he wouldn't.

Then, as Troop stopped for a look at the west slope, he glimpsed two riders, and identifying them at once, was no longer cold: Monk Monroe and Oak Creek Kirby—less than a hundred yards below him!

They were riding abreast, following his tracks northward. Now, as Troop drew his gun, Kirby pulled up, turned his back to the wind, and began making a cigarette. Monroe rode on a few feet before stopping. When he also turned his horse against the wind, Troop observed the gun in Monk's right hand. He knew then what they were up to, and knew there'd never be a better time for settlement with these two toughs. This, by God was made to order.

With a savage eagerness in him, Troop called harshly, 'Start shooting, Monk!'

Monroe's face jerked up, his startled eyes locating Troop so swiftly that both guns exploded at the same instant. The angle was bad for Monk, his bullet missing Troop by a foot or more. But Troop didn't miss. He fired twice at Monroe, and saw him double over the saddle horn with both hands clutching the front of his slicker so that he sat as if accomplishing a low and gallant bow.

Dropping his Durham sack, Oak Creek Kirby had clawed for his gun and got it out. But now, observing that Monroe was wounded, he wheeled his horse into plunging flight along the slope. Troop fired, and missed, and was remotely aware of Monroe sprawled forward with both arms around the neck of his fidgeting horse. Urging Blue to a run, Troop angled down the ridge, wanting another shot at Kirby.

It was a desperate, reckless race, both horses running wide open along the rock-studded slope. Kirby glanced over his shoulder, realized that the grulla was gaining on him, and began firing. But Troop, with only two unspent shells in his gun, held off until he saw that Kirby would soon reach a nearby stand of timber. He tried a shot, and cursed its inaccuracy. Then, less than fifty feet from Kirby and galloping abreast of him, Troop fired again.

Kirby's horse collapsed as if sledged, falling so abruptly that Oak Creek had no time to free his foot from the stirrup. Troop pulled to a sliding stop and was reloading his gun when Oak Creek yelled 'My leg is pinned! I think it's busted!'

'Good,' Troop muttered, feeling no pity.

Finished with reloading the Walker, he sat

there for a moment, watching Kirby's futile struggle to free himself. Oak Creek had clung to his gun, but he was facing downhill and couldn't move enough to see the man above him. Troop turned Blue back along his rocky bench, searching for a fit place to ride down, and now Kirby pleaded, 'Don't ride off!'

Troop laughed at him, and rode another dozen yards to a gravel slide.

'I'm pinned, I tell you!' Kirby shouted, his voice shrill with fear. 'Don't leave me to die like this!'

Easing Blue down the slide, Troop scanned the lower slope and observed Monroe, still riding doubled over, moving off toward Canteen Creek. Troop rode back along the ridge and halted directly behind Kirby and said, 'Toss your gun downslope.'

Oak Creek obeyed at once. He said, 'I thought you was leavin'. A man wouldn't have a chance, trapped like this. He could lay here for a month without bein' found.'

As Troop uncoiled the loop of his rope, Kirby suggested, 'Hook onto the horn, so's you'll get a liftin' pull.'

It took only a moment to free him. One pull of the horn-dallied rope allowed him to draw his right leg out. He grasped the muddy boot with probing fingers, muttering, 'My ankle is broke, or had sprained.'

162

'That's too bad,' Troop said, remembering how happily this man had held him for Monk Monroe's bruising fists. 'Should've been your neck.'

Oak Creek peered up at him. 'Ain't you got no pity?'

'You rate a slug in your gut, like Monroe,' Troop said rankly. 'Next time we meet you'll get it. Right in the gut.'

He was turning Blue to ride away when Kirby complained, 'It's five or six miles to town—and I can't walk.'

'Then crawl,' Troop said, and rode on.

The wind died down. The leaden clouds hung low, blanking out Rimrock Divide and the Sun Dance Hills, flattening and darkening the land so that it was like late twilight when Troop crossed Canteen Creek. He rubbed his chilled ears and saw shell ice along the sheltered west bank. Blue spooked at the ice, not wanting to step on it.

'Don't blame you for being scary,' Troop muttered, and gently spurred the grulla.

This country was enough to give a man the creeps. He wondered if Monk Monroe was still on his horse. The ape-faced bastard had needed shooting. 'It was him or me,' Troop told himself. When he turned into the Free Strip fork the first snowflakes sifted down. Big ones. They were like white moths brushing wet wings against his cheeks.

Troop tilted his hat brim low and tucked his chin into the collar of his slicker. This could be it, he thought morosely; real winter. He swung his feet free of stirrups and wriggled his cold-numbed toes. The ground was whitening ahead of him, merging with the gray gauze of falling snow. Troop shivered, and wondered if there'd be time to haul a few more loads of wood before drifts barricaded the wind-swept flats. He didn't see the wagon in the road until Blue turned out to pass it.

'Shedrow's rig,' Troop muttered, and thought at once that the mare had deserted her treasure-hunting master. Joe would have a long walk to town.

Peering through the sifting snow, Troop observed that the lines had fallen beneath a front wheel and pulled tight against the bit. That was why the old mare had stopped. Then, as he rode up close, Troop saw the huddled shape in the wagon.

'Joe!' he shouted, wondering why Sheldrow was bare-headed.

Shedrow didn't move. He sat just behind the seat with his knees pulled up and both arms wrapped tight, as if hugging himself. Troop leaned down and grasped Shedrow's snow-dusted mackinaw. But he didn't shake him. He looked at Joe's slack-jawed face and knew he was dead.

'Froze stiff,' Troop said in astonishment.

But how could that be? Why hadn't Joe got out and walked when he felt himself freezing? Why would a man just sit down and freeze to death?

Then Troop noticed the red welt on Shedrow's temple. It looked swollen, and there was another lump above it, in his sparse hair. Troop couldn't understand it. Had Joe fallen and struck his head against a boulder?

Troop got down. He put his ear close to Joe's mouth and listened, knowing Joe wasn't breathing, but listening anyway. And now, remembering his sarcasm at Canteen Creek this morning, Troop felt a gnawing regret. This man, who'd been a friend to him in time of need, was beyond helping. Troop cursed dejectedly, knowing there was nothing he could do for Joe Shedrow now.

Going to the mare's head, Troop turned her so that the front wheel cramped free of the lines. Then he picked them up, tied them to the whip stock, and said, 'Go on, mare—take him home.'

The mare plodded on down the road. The wagon's crooked wheels made two dark tracks against the thin carpet of snow. Troop sat there watching until the wagon faded into the gray gauze; then, fiercely scowling, he turned

Blue northward.

It was snowing harder when he crossed the flats east of the Borgstrom place. Troop peered ahead, thinking Fern might have lit the lamp early; but the snow was a thick curtain steadily drawing closer. The thought came to him now that he had accomplished something quite different than the search that had brought him eastward this morning. Monroe and Kirby had also gone on a search today, but he had seen them first. Otherwise he wouldn't be riding home.

Home?

Hell, he had no more home than a desert jack rabbit. But he was lucky to be riding with a whole hide. He thought, The old dame had her arm around me again.

Troop was into the yard before he saw the lighted window. Fern must have been watching for him; she opened the door as he rode past and called, 'I've got good news for you.'

Troop pulled up facing her, and wondering how any news could be good on a day like this.

'The Jersey came up to the corral at noon,' she announced smilingly, 'and brought a calf with her.'

'She did? Well, I'll be damned!'

'It's the cutest calf,' Fern said.

Afterward, at the supper table, Troop told

Fern about Joe Shedrow. 'That's what he got for all his digging—the privilege of dying alone.

'A sad thing,' Fern said soberly. 'But Mr. Shedrow had his treasure. The best part of it. The hope.'

'He got cheated all to hell,' Troop objected. 'He had his heart set on finding Curley Bill's cache and he didn't find it.'

Fern thought about that for a moment. Then the half-smiling expression came to her face and she said, 'The good of the treasure was in the seeking. He had that.'

Troop looked her in the eye. He said, 'A man needs more than the seeking. He needs the having.'

'Perhaps what he seeks is not right for him to have,' Fern suggested. Then, smiling, she went to the stove and said, 'I baked an apple pie for you.'

Troop laughed in spite of himself.

But later, when he opened the door and saw that it was still snowing, he said, 'May not be able to get another load of wood if this keeps up.'

'Perhaps we have enough,' Fern said optimistically.

'That's what folks thought the winter of the Big Die,' Troop said. 'But they found out different.'

167

Blue nickered to him when he went into the wagon shed. The grulla sounded uneasy, as if something were fretting him. 'Me too,' Troop muttered. 'I feel the same way, kid.'

If the wind came up, the snow would drift . . .

CHAPTER SIXTEEN

The snow fell steadily, silently, all night. It formed a high white frosting on the haystack; it crested the top poles of the corral and fashioned ragged blankets on the backs of mother cows that brought their calves to the fence.

Troop was up at daybreak. He trudged through ankle-deep snow to the brook that ran through the horse trap, and chopped a hole in the ice so the horses could drink. He forked hay to them and to the cows that stood hopefully at the fence. On the way to the cabin he peered eastward, wondering how much snow there'd be on the flats by late afternoon.

It was still snowing when Troop harnessed the team after breakfast. Fern came out with a shawl over her head. She placed his gunny-sacked lunch in the wagon and said worriedly, 'If the wind blows there'll be drifts.'

'Shouldn't wonder,' Troop muttered, fastening the trace chains and feeling the metal's coldness bite through his gloves.

'Perhaps you shouldn't go,' Fern suggested.

Troop climbed into the wagon. He stood behind the seat and looked down at her and said, 'A man can't expect it to be summer all the time.'

Fern smiled at that. She called, 'Good luck,' and waved to him as he drove out of the yard.

The wheels made a crunching sound against the dry snow. Smoky puffs jetted from the horses' nostrils. Troop rubbed his ears and stomped his feet against the plank wagon bed and wondered how cold it was now. Must be ten below, by the feel of it. He took off his hat and tied a neckerchief over his head so that it shielded his ears, then pulled the hat down over it.

'Part winter and part summer,' he scoffed, recalling Fern's talk.

Words. That's all they were; just nice-sounding words.

They didn't sound so nice out here with frost stinging your nostrils and the cold biting through your boots. He wondered why Fern's talk had made him feel ashamed—as if he were a Gentle Annie wanting to dodge something he shouldn't. The way she said it, you'd think he was afraid of winter.

'Afraid, hell,' Troop muttered. He didn't like snow, was all.

Then a curious thought came to him: Maybe he *was* afraid, with a sort of spooky fear, like Blue felt when he saw the ice at Canteen Creek. Something instinctive, the way animals feared certain things.

Troop stomped his feet. He held the lines against his side and smacked his gloved hands to warm them. He noticed that the wind was blowing. Not hard, but enough to slant the dry snow so that it no longer sifted straight down. Wouldn't take much wind to pile up drifts, he reflected. This might be the beginning of the blizzard he'd been predicting. Troop was tempted to turn back. He could put in the day chopping stovewood and stacking it against the cabin's west wall.

He thought, It will be worse, coming back with a load. And he would be facing the wind.

A man had a right to be afraid of weather like this. But stronger than his fear was a compelling need to show Fern Borgstrom that he could take winter as well as the next man. And so he kept going.

The snow was shin-deep when Troop reached the timbered ridge, and now an increasing wind whimpered through the pines. The team was restless, disliking the wind-driven snow. He tied the horses to a tree, not trusting them to stand, and got busy with the ax. Chopping was a welcome chore to him now; it warmed his body and eased his mind. One more load of logs would make a month's supply of firewood on hand. He was trimming out his second tree when he saw Joe Maffitt riding toward him with his right hand held up Indian-fashion.

The Slash C rider halted part way down the ridge. He peered from the ample protection of a sheepskin's upturned collar and called, 'You seen anything of Dade?'

Troop shook his head, wondering about this, and now Maffitt announced, 'We was lookin' for Monk. His horse came home last night with blood smeared all over the saddle. I just found Monk over yonderly by the creek.'

'Dead?'

'Cold dead and covered with snow. How about lendin' me your wagon to tote him into town?'

'Hell, no,' Troop said. 'Just rope Monk's boots and drag him in.'

Maffitt complained, 'That's no way to treat a corpse.'

'Then tote him on your goddamn back,' Troop said rankly.

Joe turned to leave, then asked, 'You seen Oak Creek?'

'Yeah. He was crawling toward town on his hands and knees.'

'When was that?' Maffitt asked solemnly.

'Yesterday afternoon.'

Joe peered at him a moment longer, then said, 'I always knowed you was downright hazardous.'

Then he rode back down the ridge.

Troop watched him until he disappeared in the snow-pelted willows along the creek. Joe wasn't very bright, thinking he'd get the loan of a wagon on a day like this. Troop wondered where Chastain was riding, and thought, I'll have to keep my eyes peeled for that jigger.

At noon, when he stopped to eat his lunch, Troop noticed that there was a knee-deep drift on the west side of the wagon. He could scarcely see the team for wind-swirled snow. Instead of eating, he began loading the logs already cut. The snow would be drifting on the flats.

Halfway down the ridge Troop got off and walked beside the wagon. The wind seemed stronger now, more bitter cold. It went right through his pants. Remembering that Fern had offered him Swede's overcoat, he cursed himself for refusing to wear a dead man's garment. That old overcoat would feel damn good right now.

Presently Troop got back on the wagon and

peered into the mealy gloom ahead. They were on the flats now, and he didn't want to miss the road. But the windslanted snow blinded him. Unable to get his bearings, Troop gave the horses their heads, allowing them to choose their own course, and hoping they'd find the road. There was an arroyo that had to be crossed at the right place or they'd never get past it.

The team lunged into a drift, whipsawed in momentary confusion as the wagon's front wheels stuck, then floundered through. The next drift was deeper. The horses sulked, refusing to pull until Troop lashed their rumps with the lines. They leaned into their collars then, clawed for footing, and pulled together. But they couldn't budge the wagon.

Troop cursed, and threw off three logs. He backed the horses a wagon length, then lashed them forward. They got through the drift and plodded across a wind-swept stretch of bare ground.

The wind made a shrill continuous wailing. All the coldness that Lew Troop hated was in it; a slashing saber-sharp coldness that chilled him to the bone. The team stalled in another drift. Troop threw off three logs again, then three more. Thr horses lunged forward into snow that became constantly deeper, and soon stopped again. Troop tossed the last of his load into that drift; he stood in the empty wagon and danced a jig to keep his feet from freezing. And because Troop saw this as an ironic joke, he shouted ribald laughter into the wind. It seemed comical that Lew Troop, who had shunned snow as other men shunned smallpox, should be slowly freezing out here on the Free Strip flats.

The team stalled again. Troop lashed their frosty backs and yelled curses that were lost in the wind's shrill howling. Again and again he urged the horses into frantic effort, angling them gee and haw.

'Pull, you bastards! Pull!'

But the wagon didn't budge.

The wind was a high thin wailing. There was a sadness in it and a droning futility. Troop got down. He turned his back to the wind and tried to roll a cigarette. But his fingers were too cold. They were like thumbs. Sore thumbs. He shrugged, and flipped the torn cigarette paper into the wind. It wasn't important whether he smoked or not. Losing the load of logs wasn't important either. Nothing was important.

This, Troop supposed, was how Joe Shedrow felt yesterday when he sat down to die. As if it didn't make much difference. He peered at the snow-blurred horses. They stood with heads bowed against the storm, and he thought, They don't care either. He wondered if they could get through the drift without the wagon. The snow was up to their bellies now.

Working with cold-numbed hands, Troop unhitched the trace chains. Then, clinging to the lines, he shouted at the team. The horses went forward in a lunge that yanked Troop off his feet. He got up, and fell again, and was dragged along on his belly. It would have been easy to let go of the lines. Easier than clinging to them. But for some obscure reason that he couldn't identify, Troop chose to hang on. When the team finally halted he got to his feet, believing they were stuck in another drift.

'Go on, you bastards!' he screeched. 'Drag me some more!'

But the horses just stood there, and now Troop saw what had stopped them. They were standing in front of the wagon shed.

Slowly, in the deliberate fashion of a man accomplishing a difficult chore, Troop opened the corral gate. Blue nickered a greeting from the shed's sheltered gloom; the Jersey and her white-faced calf eyed him solemnly. The wind whined above the shed and around it, but this end of the corral was sheltered. It was like a snug harbor against the storm.

Troop was in the wagon shed unharnessing the horses when Fern hurried in with a blanket draped squaw-fashion over her head. 'Are you all right?' she asked in a more excited voice than he'd ever heard her use.

Troop nodded. 'Had to leave the wagon. Snow got a trifle too deep.'

'I was afraid you wouldn't start back in time,' Fern said. 'I'd about made up my mind to saddle Blue and come looking for you when Mr. Chastain arrived.'

'Chastain?'

Fern nodded.

'What'd he want?' Troop asked.

'Well, he started out to search for two of his men who were missing. He broke his left leg when his horse fell off a cut bank. The horse got away from him. It must have been awful— out in such a storm, and crippled. He was half frozen when he crawled up to the door dragging his broken leg.'

For a moment, as Troop absorbed that news, he peered at her in squint-eyed wonderment. Then he loosed a hoot of gusty laughter, and leaning against the shed wall, laughed like a man beside himself with glee.

'What's so comical?' Fern demanded.

'You,' Troop said, pointing a finger at her. 'The Free Strip woman who causes Texas saddle bums to buck blizzards, and nester-hating cattlemen to come crawling to her doorstep. What could be more comical than that?'

But Fern didn't see the humor of it, for she said, 'It won't be necessary for you to buck another blizzard, Lew.'

She turned and went quickly back across the snow-pelted yard.

Troop chuckled. That was just like a woman. Worried for fear you wouldn't make it, then get huffy because you felt like laughing. Troop fed the horses. When he went into his bunk room he felt let down and exhausted. Pulling off his boots, he got into bed, thinking he would take a little time to warm up gradually before going to the cabin.

It would be odd, eating supper with Dade Chastain—with the cranky bastard who'd sent two men gunning for him yesterday. But it would be good to watch Chastain accept favors from the woman he'd tried to run off this place.

The wind pushed hard against the wagon shed, making roof timbers creak; it drove snow between the warped boards and made a shrill whine around the eaves. But the blankets warmed Troop; a pleasant drowsiness came with the warmth, and he decided to take a short nap. A man got tired, tromping through snowdrifts. He got tired as hell . . .

It was morning when Troop awoke. He had

no way of knowing that Fern had looked in on him at suppertime and decided not to disturb him. He thought she had forgotten all about her hired man, or if she had remembered his presence, hadn't taken the trouble to call him for supper.

'Must be sore about something,' Troop muttered, and wondered if it were because he'd laughed at her. Well, it *was* comical, the way things had turned out.

Troop pulled on his cold-stiffened boots. The wind was still blowing, and snow sifted through the cracks of the shed's west wall. A real blizzard, and no telling how long it would last. He'd have to get some stovewood stacked where it would be handy for Fern. But first of all he'd take on some food. He felt, by God, as if he hadn't eaten for a week.

CHAPTER SEVENTEEN

Dade Chastain sat in the rocker with his injured leg propped on the barrel chair. He looked up as Troop came in; he asked, 'Still snowing?'

Troop nodded.

'Did you get your sleep out?' Fern asked, toting a skillet of fried potatoes to the table

There was something about her voice and the way she glanced at him that puzzled Troop. Not as if she were displeased, or resentful about anything. But different. . . .

He said, 'A real good sleep,' and watched her go back to the stove. Her hair was done up exactly as it had been yesterday, and she wore the same dress. But there was a change in her that he couldn't identify.

Fern poured his coffee. She pointed to a china pitcher, saying, 'Fresh cream for your coffee. I milked the Jersey.'

'Did she put up a fight?' Troop asked.

'No. I fed her some grain and she stood quiet. Jerseys are like that.'

Troop glanced over at Chastain. Dade had been watching him, and now they looked at each other in frowning silence until Chastain asked, 'Did you shoot Monk Monroe?'

Troop nodded.

'Monk must've fallen off and died somewhere on the way home,' Chastain said matter-of-factly. 'Oak Creek too?'

'Just his horse.'

Ignoring Chastain's continuing appraisal, Troop went on with his eating. Dade seemed different, too. Sort of subdued. The broken leg might account for that, but not for the change in Fern. When Troop looked at Chastain and found Dade peering at him he asked, 'Why you gawking at me?'

'Just trying to figure something out,' Chastain said, very mild about this. 'I thought you got by because you were lucky. But now I guess it's more than that. I guess it's because you just don't give a damn.' Then Dade did an odd thing. He held up a hand and said to Fern, 'Excuse me, ma'am. I'm not accustomed to having ladies present.'

'I've heard worse,' Fern murmured, giving Troop a sidelong glance.

Troop couldn't understand it. Dade Chastain apologizing to a homestead woman. It seemed past believing. And it wasn't just the words he'd used, but the tone of his voice—so meek and mild you'd mistake him for a grubline bum thankful for a handout.

'You sound,' Troop scoffed, 'like you'd been reading a Bible.'

Chastain shook his head. 'I'm just grateful, is all. A man caught in a blizzard with a busted leg does a deal of thinking. He worries about freezing to death, or being a gimpy-legged cripple for the rest of his life. Well, I won't be, thanks to Miss Borgstrom. No medico could have set and splinted my leg better than she did.'

Troop stared at him. This couldn't be Dade Chastain. Not the crusty bastard who'd bossed Cathedral Basin like a brass-riveted

180

king.

'You must've had hell scared out of you,' Troop mused. 'How far did you drag that leg?'

'Upwards of three miles,' Chastain said. He grimaced, adding, 'It was the worst thing I ever went through. Not just the pain. But the cold, and knowing I'd freeze unless I got to a fire.'

He looked at Fern and smiled. The smile changed his face so completely that he seemed strange to Troop, like a younger brother of Dade Chastain. It even warmed his bleached-blue eyes and mellowed his voice as he said, 'No fire ever felt good as this one, ma'am—and none ever will.'

Troop couldn't understand it. How could a man so goddamn mean change so much in one day's time? It was loco as a drunkard's dream. But Fern didn't seem surprised. She looked as if she'd known all along that Chastain would be like this. Recalling what she had said about Dade, he marveled at the exact way she had tallied the Slash C boss. There was a flaw of downright softness in Chastain—a woman-wanting flaw, most likely. And Fern had been keen enough to detect it.

Troop smiled at her. 'You've got sharp eyes,' he mused.

'What makes you say that?' she asked.

181

'Because you see things that no one else even suspected.'

She was standing at the stove, waiting for the coffee to warm. Color stained her cheeks as he continued his admiring appraisal, and now he teased, 'Why are you blushing?'

As if talking to himself, Chastain mused, 'It was a lucky thing for me that Swede built his cabin here. Otherwise I would've froze to death.'

'It beats all what one busted leg will do to a man,' Troop said.

Fern was pouring him a second cup of coffee when Chastain announced, 'I've asked Miss Borgstrom to be my wife.'

'Wife!' Troop echoed.

He stared at Chastain in frank astonishment and demanded, 'You—marry her?'

Chastain nodded, and now Fern asked, 'Does that surprise you?'

'So that's it,' Troop muttered. That was why Fern had seemed different. She'd been proposed to; pleaded with, most likely, by a man who owned the biggest ranch in Cathedral Basin. Now there'd be no doubt about getting that monument to her father.

'Is it odd that a man should want to marry me?' Fern demanded.

Troop forced a grin. 'It would be odd if a man didn't want to marry you.'

182

Fern studied him intently for a moment. She seemed on the verge of asking a question. Then she shrugged and turned to Chastain, and refilled his coffee cup.

Troop continued with his breakfast. He told himself that it was no skin off his nose who she married. But it didn't seem right, regardless. Chastain was too old for her. Too dried up, and set in his ways. An old man's ways. Fern should have a younger husband, Troop thought, and was remotely aware of their conversation. Once he heard her say in a thoroughly pleased voice, 'It will mean so much to so many people.'

Yes, Troop thought, this new setup on the Free Strip would mean a great deal to folks wanting homesteads in Cathedral Basin. And it meant a lot to him also. He was no longer needed here. Fern wouldn't want a hired man; she'd have the Slash C crew to do her bidding. And with Dade Chastain gone soft over a woman, there'd be no matter of a drifter's pride involved. He could ride south soon as the storm let up enough so Blue could travel.

So thinking, Troop reached for his hat and said, 'Reckon I'll chop some firewood.'

'There's no need to hurry,' Fern said.

Chastain didn't speak. He sat there looking at Fern, like a man dreaming with his eyes open.

The wind died down during the morning. Fern came out and said optimistically, 'I think the storm is over.'

'Seems like,' Troop agreed, continuing to swing the ax.

She toted two armfuls of firewood and presently shoveled a path to the privy. Afterward, when Troop stopped to roll a cigarette, he observed Chastain hobbling along the path on a homemade crutch. Dade didn't look much like the boss of a big warrior outfit now; hopping along with his broken leg held up and both hands grasping the crutch, he looked more like some crippled old homesteader.

It was still snowing at dusk, but when Troop fed the mother cows he noticed that the snow had melted off their backs. The weather was warming up. If the wind didn't blow again there'd be a chance of riding out of here in a day or two. Fern didn't need a hired man now, and he'd seen all the goddamn snow he ever wanted to see. If the stage road south was open, he could be out of it in two days' riding.

Chastain was already seated at the supper table when Troop went into the cabin. The Slash C boss seemed oddly cheerful for a man with a broken leg. He praised Fern's cooking, telling her he hadn't eaten such fine fare since leaving home thirty years ago. When she passed him a piece of apple pie Chastain smacked his lips and announced, 'I'm glad that pony fell with me, ma'am!'

Troop watched Fern's smiling acceptance of Chastain's praise and resented it. The way she acted, you'd think Dade was the answer to a woman's prayer—that she could scarcely wait to marry the crippled old devil. By God, it was enough to turn a man's stomach.

It occurred to Troop then that he was jealous. And that made him all the more resentful. He had always considered jealous men one notch lower than sheepherders. There were plenty of women to go around; no reason for a man to make a fool of himself over any one of them. If Fern wanted her monument enough to marry Chastain, that was her business and none of his.

But he couldn't think down the resentment, and it was worse at breakfast next morning with Dade so cheerful and soft with his talk. The thought came to Troop that he'd never really hated Dade Chastain. Even though he had despised the man, he'd never hated him. But he did now—so thoroughly that the food he ate almost gagged him.

Getting up from the table, Troop said to Fern, 'I'm leaving as of right now.'

She didn't speak. She just looked up at him with wide, startled eyes, and Chastain

185

demanded. 'What's all the rush?'

Troop ignored him. He put on his hat and was opening the door when Fern asked, 'Do you think there'd be a chance of reaching Signal with the wagon today?'

'Not unless you shoveled through the drifts,' Troop said. 'What's your hurry?'

'Well, I'd like to have a doctor look at Mr. Chastain's leg. I think the bone is set properly, but I'd like to be sure—before it begins to knit. If it should happen to be crooked, the bone would have to be broken all over again.'

Chastain said, 'The only bad drifts will be between here and the stage road. You could ride along with us and shovel those out.'

'No,' Troop said.

'Why not?' Chastain demanded.

'Because I'm sick of the sight of you,' Troop said rankly. 'It turns my stomach just to look at you.'

Then he said to Fern, 'I'll bring the wagon in. I'll tote a shovel along and open up the drifts. But you'd better wait until tomorrow morning, so you'll have all day to make the trip.'

Fern seemed pleased. She smiled and said, 'I'm very grateful, Lew.'

It took Troop upwards of an hour to get the wagon dug out and pulled into the yard. Then he saddled Blue, and observing that the front cinch ring had cut part way through the worn leather supporting it, he thought, I'll have to get it fixed in town. When he rode across the yard Fern was waiting for him on the stoop.

'*Adios*, sorrel-top,' Troop said, halting in front of her. 'Don't reckon you'll ever need another hired man.'

Fern held up a handful of silver dollars. 'Here's the money I owe you, in addition to much gratitude. I don't suppose you'd stay, even if I asked you.'

'Not with a monument-maker in the house,' Troop muttered, and motioned the money aside.

'But you must take it,' Fern insisted. 'Think how hard you worked—all the wood you chopped.'

Troop shook his head. 'Just a favor for a lady, is all.'

'I'd rather you took the money,' Fern told him. Then she asked, 'Are you going to stay overnight in town?'

'Depends on what time I get there. And if Lee Monroe still wants to square up for that busted beak I gave him.' Troop grinned, remembering. Dame Fortune and Belle Smith both had their arms around him that night.

Fern frowned. 'Why don't you ride around Signal?' she suggested, very insistent about this. 'Why risk more trouble when it isn't necessary? You could ride along a back street and they wouldn't see you at all.'

Troop laughed at her. 'What you take me for—a homesteader?' he scoffed.

'No, Lew,' she said soberly. 'You'd never be a homesteader. You couldn't change that much.'

Her voice was low and throaty, as it had been that first day he met her. The subdued tone of it was in perfect harmony with her high-boned cheeks and sweet curving lips. As he looked at those lips now, it occurred to Troop that he had not kissed her, and that this was the last chance he would ever have. The need to kiss her this one time was an impulse so strong he couldn't resist it. Leaning over swiftly, he took her in his arms. He lifted her and kissed her, long and hard.

For a timeless interval, while the wild sweet flavor of her lips merged with the woman fragrance of her hair, Troop held Fern free of the ground. Until she protested, 'Lew—you're hurting me!'

He released her at once, seeing the warm wetness of her eyes, the rose glow that flooded her cheeks.

'You're not cold,' he said, and felt like grabbing her again, but she backed away. He shrugged. 'Well, I've got that much to

188

remember.'

Then he angled over to the wagon, picked up the shovel, and rode out of the yard without looking back.

CHAPTER EIGHTEEN

Each drift seemed deeper to Troop. He shoveled and sweated and cursed himself for making such a fool deal. He could have been in Signal and bellied up to the Shamrock bar by noon if he hadn't promised to dig through the drifts. At the rate he was going, he'd be lucky to reach town by dark. And all this goddamn toil for a woman who was going to marry Dade Chastain. What a joke that was— Fern Borgstrom marrying a crusty old cattleman who had hounded her father off his homestead.

A hell of a joke, all right. But not the kind you laughed at. A man would have to be real drunk to see the funny side of it.

Troop had dug through three hip-high drifts when he observed two riders, blackly etched against the vast whiteness, approaching from the east. Lancing the shovel into a drift, he drew his gun.

Big Bill Eggleston and Joe Maffitt, he

guessed. They were probably searching for Chastain; two hired hands looking for their boss. And they'd want no fuss with a Texas drifter who had a gun in his fist.

Presently, as they came close enough to confirm his guess, an idea occurred to Troop. An idea that made him grin. Dame Fortune, he thought now, still had her arm around him.

Observing Troop's gun, Eggleston called, 'We ain't after you,' and coming on with both hands in plain sight, the sheriff announced, 'We're lookin' for Dade. He ain't at the ranch. We figgered he might of holed up at Swede's place.'

'He did,' Troop said.

Joe Maffitt glanced at Eggleston. He muttered, 'We should of come here first, like I told you.'

Big Bill paid Joe no heed. He peered at Troop and asked solemnly, 'Is Dade alive?'

Troop nodded. 'But he's got a busted leg. That's why I was digging out the drifts, so a wagon could get through.' He nodded at the upright shovel and grinned and said, 'Now you jiggers can do the digging while I take my ease in town.'

Eggleston nudged back his hat, plainly dismayed at the thought of so tedious a chore. 'You're Miss Borgstrom's hired man, Lew. Seems like it's your job to clear her road.'

'I'm not her hired man any more,' Troop said. 'But you are—both of you.'

'What you mean by that?' Joe Maffitt demanded.

Troop grinned, enjoying this. 'Go ask Chastain,' he suggested.

'What's Dade got to do with us bein' a homestead woman's hired men?' Big Bill asked. 'It don't make sense.'

'Dade will explain it,' Troop promised, and as they rode around him he asked, 'Is Lee Monroe in town?'

'He sure is,' Maffitt reported, 'and he's all broke up about Monk. Says he'll git you if it's the last thing he ever does.'

Troop grinned and said, 'It might be, if he tries it.' Then he asked, 'Did they bury Joe Shedrow?'

'The next morning after the mare brung him in,' Eggleston said. Then he turned in the saddle and demanded, 'How'd you know about Shedrow dying?'

'None of your goddamn business,' Troop said. Impatient now to be on his way, he waggled the gun and ordered, 'Get going. Go on to Swede's place and meet your new boss.'

Troop held Blue there in the trail until Eggleston and Maffitt were out of pistol range; then he rode eastward with a pleasant sense of anticipation in him. He would be in

191

town by noon, and riding the south stage road soon afterward. Recalling what Maffitt had said about Lee Monroe, Troop shrugged. The mule-skinner might take a sneak shot at a man after dark, but he wouldn't face him in daylight. Monroe had a yellow streak.

When Troop crossed Canteen Creek he remembered how he'd first seen Fern here; how she'd made him itch, just looking at her. It seemed like a long time ago, so much had happened since then. He recalled how queenly she'd looked, sitting there on the wagon's spring seat; how calm and confident she'd been.

Troop muttered, 'Got to forget I ever met her.'

He tried to shut her out of his mind, and knew dismally that he never would. There was no way to keep your thoughts from sliding back; to keep from finding a woman's face half hidden in a heap of discarded memories. First there'd be just the face—a blurred image of warm eyes and full lips and high-boned cheeks with a half-smiling expression on them. But you'd remember other things that made it more than an image: the wild sweet flavor of her lips, the soft touch of slim fingers, and the woman smell of her. You'd remember how she had knelt in a dusty road and let soil trickle from her cupped palm and said, 'It is good.'

You'd remember all the nice things. And then you'd think about her being married to Dade Chastain; how she had traded herself for a monument to the memory of Swede Borgstrom.

Again, as it had last night while he lay on his bunk and couldn't sleep, the enormity of it confounded Troop. Fern Borgstrom had deliberately sold herself. Even though it wasn't for money, it amounted to the same thing. She had sold herself just as surely as some skirt-lifting trollop bartering her body for profit.

It seemed past believing. But it was so...

The snow wasn't so deep east of Canteen Creek. There were many patches of bare ground and no drifts worth mentioning. The storm, Troop supposed, had centered over Rimrock divide and spent itself on the Free Strip flats. There probably was no snow to speak of on the south stage road, and now, as the sun shone through a big rift in the clouds, he said to Blue, 'A good day for traveling, kid.'

When Troop rode into Signal shortly after noon the sun's warmth had set eaves to dripping and Main Street was hoof-deep in muddy slush. Turning into Ledbetter's Livery, Troop unsaddled and ordered a double ration of oats for the grulla. He was going out, toting the saddle on his left shoulder, when Ike Ledbetter warned, 'Better keep an eye peeled for Lee Monroe.'

'Has he got a gun?' Troop asked.

Ledbetter nodded and said, 'He's been target practicin' out behind my manure pile for three days straight. Must of shot off half a dozen boxes of shells. Never saw a man do so much shootin'.'

'So,' Troop mused. He gave Main Street a questing appraisal and asked, 'How'd he do, Ike?'

'Real good, after Oak Creek Kirby started coachin' him. That Kirby knows all the tricks.'

'I thought Oak Creek broke his leg,' Troop muttered.

'Just a sprained ankle, is all. But it's Monroe you want to watch out for, Lew. He's told everybody in town that he's goin' to gun you down on sight.'

'Front or back?' Troop inquired cynically.

Ledbetter smiled and said, 'He didn't say. But he's proddy enough to try it either way.'

Troop thought about that as he went on along the plank walk toward Wimple's Saddle Shop. It didn't seem likely that Monroe would make a stand-up fight, even though he'd made big brags; but if his target practicing had

194

given the mule-skinner enough courage, he might give it a try.

Oak Creek Kirby came out of the Shamrock Saloon, across the street. He called, 'Hello, Troop,' with a surprising show of friendliness, and went limping along the sidewalk.

Troop, nearly to the Palacial Hotel now, watched Kirby go into the Chink's Café. There was something odd about that genial greeting from a man who had every reason to dislike him. Especially odd, considering that Oak Creek had helped Monroe improve his shooting.

Abruptly then, Troop understood that Kirby hadn't greeted him because of friendliness; the gimpy rider had used that method of telling Lee Monroe that his target was in town. The mule-skinner, Troop guessed, was in the saloon. And at this same moment, as Troop came abreast of the Palacial, Belle Smith hurried down the veranda steps.

'Lew!' she exclaimed, 'What are you doing in town?'

'On my way south,' Troop said, warily watching the Shamrock batwings. 'Got to get my saddle repaired.'

'You mean you're all through at Swede's place?'

Troop nodded, not looking at her until she

195

asked, 'Was I right about her, Lew?'

'Well, not exactly,' Troop said, and grinned at her. 'Miss Borgstrom gave me something.'

'What?'

'All the apple pie I could eat.'

Belle liked that. She said smilingly, 'I shouldn't of lost my temper that night, Lew. I been sorry for the way I acted. Awful sorry. Can we be good friends again?'

She had a kiss-me look in her eyes now, an invitation a man couldn't mistake; the warm, bright-eyed look of a woman wanting to be wanted. She wore a dress that fitted snugly at her waist, emphasizing the swell of firm, full breasts, and the way she waited, with a smile parting her moist lips, stirred an elemental hunger in Troop. But because Joe Shedrow had been his good friend, Troop asked, 'How does it feel to be a widow?'

Belle's expression changed instantly. 'I'm real sorry Joe died likc he did,' she murmured, very sober about this. 'But I guess we just weren't meant for each other, the way a husband and wife should be.'

'Joe thought a lot of you,' Troop said. 'That's why he wanted to find the Curly Bill cache—so he could buy all the fancy knicknacks you wanted.'

Belle shrugged and said, 'Joe was treasure-loco.'

Then her eyes widened and she exclaimed, 'Look out, Lew! Here comes Lee Monroe!'

And in this same instant, the mule-skinner shouted, 'Grab your gun, saddle tramp!'

CHAPTER NINETEEN

Troop pushed Belle Smith away from him and said, 'Go on, girl! Go on!'

He stood motionless as she backed off, knowing that Monroe would fire the moment he turned, and wanting Belle out of the way. Monroe didn't need to shoot him in the back; the mule-skinner could fake a fair fight now, and still have all the best of it.

'Turn around!' Monroe shouted.

The sunlight was warm against Troop's neck. Perspiration dripped from his armpits and his face felt hot, as if he were running a fever. But tension tied a cold knot in his stomach as he watched Belle back away from him.

Troop shifted the weight of the saddle on his shoulder, intending to let the heavy gear drop. But a thought came to him now; an idea that formed a fragile strand of hope for survival. Monroe, he understood, would draw and fire the moment he turned. There wasn't a chance of beating the mule-skinner's first shot. Or the second one, either. But if he had a little luck with the saddle . . .

So thinking, Troop drew and whirled and yanked the saddle across his chest in one swift flow of desperate motion.

Belle Smith saw Monroe's gun dart up and explode twice as Troop turned. She saw Troop rock back on his heels as if hard hit, but her high-pitched scream was drowned out by the blast of Troop's gun merging with Monroe's third shot.

It was an odd thing. An unbelievable thing. Belle saw Troop rock back, as if hit again. Yet he didn't go down. He stood there, tall and gaunt and bitter-eyed, still holding to his saddle. He peered at Lee Monroe, who now took a floundering step forward. The gun dropped from Monroe's hand and clattered onto the saloon stoop, the sound seeming loud against the street's sudden hush. Monroe bowed his head. He made one grab for a stoop post and missed it and tipped slowly over.

Belle could scarcely believe it. 'He shot three times and you're alive,' she marveled, hurrying up to Troop. 'You shot once and he's dead.'

'Luck,' Troop muttered. 'Pure luck.'

Then, seeing Kirby come out of the café doorway, Troop called, 'How about you, Oak

Creek?'

Kirby shook his head. He peered at Monroe's sprawled form and then stared hard at Troop, demanding, 'Didn't he hit you at all?'

'Not a scratch,' Troop said.

Matt Shayne came out to look at Monroe. 'He was drinkin' me best whisky not five minutes ago,' the old Irishman proclaimed. 'Now look at him—shot through the heart. And him one of my best customers. 'Tis a cryin' shame, bejasus—a cryin' shame!'

'Men are born to violence,' Doc Pendergast announced. He elbowed his way through the ring of morbid spectators, commanding, 'Make way for the coroner.'

Troop holstered his gun. 'I guess that settles the score,' he sighed.

Belle plucked his sleeve. 'You look tired, honey. You look like you'd been drug through a knot hole by the heels. Come on up to my room and rest yourself.'

'It's an idea,' Troop mused, thinking now that it was good for a man to be wanted. And not because of a monument, or because he was handy at raising crops. It was good to be wanted just because he was a man—the way Belle wanted him.

'Let's go upstairs,' Belle urged, 'where folks can't gawk at you.'

Troop hadn't been aware of it, but now he observed that they were all looking at him. He heard a woman somewhere behind him say, 'That's Lew Troop, the tough Texan who killed both the Monroes. I wouldn't be surprised if he had something to do with Joe Shedrow's death, too.'

A self-mocking grin rutted Troop's gaunt cheeks. He said to Belle, 'It wouldn't be fitting for you to be seen going into the hotel with a tough Texan. I'll take this saddle into Wimple's and maybe come up later.'

'For sure?' Belle asked.

Troop shrugged, not sure of anything. He watched two men tote Monroe's body along the street. He said, 'I don't know.'

'But you're going to stay in town tonight, aren't you?'

'Depends on how long it takes to fix this saddle,' Troop said. 'I want to get out of this goddamn country before another snowstorm hits.'

An old man wearing a shabby mackinaw and bib overalls stepped up to Troop and asked, 'Is Miss Borgstrom still livin' at Swede's old place?'

'Yes, if it's any of your business,' Troop said, and walked on to where Pop Wimple stood in his doorway.

The saddle maker backed into the shop and

asked, 'Did those bullets hit your saddle, son?'

'All three of them,' Troop said. He lowered the saddle to Wimple's work bench and peered at the bullet holes. Two of the slugs had ripped through a bucking roll and were imbedded in the cantle. A third bullet had penetrated the leather-covered hull; when Wimple upended the saddle Troop saw the lead slug protruding from the sheepskin lining.

'That one came close,' he mused. 'God-awful close.'

'Lucky you was fetchin' the saddle to me,' Wimple said. 'Otherwise you'd of been a gone goose for sure.'

Troop nodded. He pointed to the cinch ring and asked, 'How long will it take to put in a new hanger?'

'Half an hour or so,' Wimple said

'I'll wait,' Troop said, and he stood in the doorway, idly watching the crowd disperse. It occurred to him that he'd had a full share of luck out there today. More luck than most men ever had. He should be feeling high as a windmill. A man who'd felt the impact of three bullets without getting hurt had something to feel high about; something to celebrate. But because the tension had run out, leaving him mired in a backwash of bleak futility, Troop didn't even want a drink. He wondered if Fern would bring Chastain into town today, or wait until tomorrow. That would be something for folks to gawk at—Dade Chastain riding with Swede Borsgrom's daughter!

And the wedding? . . .

Troop cursed, thinking what a grand affair that would be, with the whole town invited.

The old man in the tattered mackinaw came up to him and asked meekly, 'Do you suppose there'd be a chance for me on the Strip, Mr. Troop?'

'Yes,' Troop said indifferently.

The swift brightening of hope in the homesteader's eyes reminded Troop of Joe Shedrow, and so he said, 'There'll be no more trouble on the Free Strip.'

'You mean—Dade Chastain is dead?' the old man asked.

'The one you knew is,' Troop said, and because this man eyed him in wonderment, he added, 'Chastain has changed his mind about keeping folks off the Free Strip.'

'By grab!' the old man blurted, hugely pleased. 'Joe Shedrow said it would happen. He told us we'd all have places out there come spring. But we could scarcely believe him.'

Then he swung around and waved to another shabby man farther along the street and shouted, 'I got news for you, George! Real good news!'

It didn't take much to please some men, Troop reflected sourly. All the sodbuster wanted was a chance to work his fool head off on foot. A witless breed, thankful for the privilege of scratching out a bare living.

'Good news,' Troop said, and laughed mockingly.

But he wasn't laughing when he rode Blue out of the livery half an hour later. He thought, Another town behind me, and saw with stark clarity how it would always be for him. A few weeks' work breaking another man's broncs, or rounding up another man's cattle; a winter in some lonely line camp on the desert, a summer rimming the high country. Year after wandering year of it . . .

He was passing the Palacial when Belle called to him from the lobby doorway. He angled over to the sidewalk as she came down the steps. He was sorry she had seen him.

'Weren't you even going to say good-by?' Belle demanded poutingly.

Troop grinned down at her. 'Sure,' he said, and tipped his hat in gallant fashion. 'Good-by, Belle—and good luck.'

'When will I see you again, Lew?'

Looking at her now, Troop knew there was no reason for them to meet again. He understood that the fun of their brief friendship was finished—gone flat and colorless as last summer's grass. There'd been a time when a pretty face and a little fun was all he wanted; all he needed. But it wasn't like that any more.

'When, Lew?'

Troop's high shoulders lifted and dropped in a shrug. With that simple expression of futility he rode away from her.

The land south of town was bare of snow. Bare and bleak as his dismal thoughts. Troop shaped up a cigarette and smoked it as the grulla shuffled along the muddy stage road. Fern Borgstrom had got what she wanted. There'd been no doubt about it in her mind, he thought; even when things looked their worst, Fern's calm confidence hadn't wavered. She had set her heart on opening the Free Strip to settlement, and she'd done it. Recalling the bright-shining hope he'd seen in the old homesteader's eyes, Troop thought, Maybe it was worth the price she's going to pay.

There'd be half a hundred families living on the Free Strip in another year. They'd make a fine monument to the memory of Swede Borgstrom. A living monument.

Presently, riding up the long dugway that cut through Signal Butte, Troop heard a

204

remote clatter of hoofbeats behind him. He glanced back, idly curious, and saw that the oncoming rider was a woman whose skirts billowed out behind her.

Belle Smith, he thought, and cursed, dreading the chore of saying good-by to her a second time. Why the hell couldn't she leave well enough alone? He'd as good as told her that he didn't want to see her again.

'Wait for me, Lew?' she called.

But it wasn't Belle Smith's voice.

Troop whirled the grulla around and saw who it was and couldn't believe it. Fern Borgstrom wouldn't do a thing like this. She wouldn't ride after a man with her skirts flapping above her knees like some Sonora camp follower. But here she was, wearing a heavy coat with a green muffler wrapped like a hood over her head.

'Where you going?' Troop demanded.

Fern pushed her skirts down. Her wind-burned cheeks were stained cherry red, and for a moment she looked at him intently, not smiling or speaking. Then she said, 'That's for you to say.'

Troop stared at her. 'You mean—'

But he couldn't finish it. He couldn't voice so fantastic a notion.

Fern nodded.

'But what about the monument to Swede?'

205

Troop demanded.

'It will be there, regardless, Lew. Mr Chastain promised me that, whether I married him or not.'

Troop peered at her in stubborn disbelief. None of this made sense to him. He asked, 'Where'd you get the horse?'

'Borrowed it from Sheriff Eggleston when I learned you'd already left town.'

She made an open-palmed gesture of resignation. 'I tried not to want you, Lew. I told myself it wouldn't work out—that you'd be a fiddle-footed husband, always wanting to look over the next hill. At least I thought you might change, and hoped you would. I even prayed that you'd change. But you didn't.'

She gave him a half-angry, accusing glance, and now, as Troop moved up close to her, she said, 'After you left I kept remembering how it was when you kissed me.'

Troop grinned. He said, 'I remember how it was, too,' and looked at her lips. They were gently smiling, and the fragrance of her hair was like a familiar perfume. She met his gaze directly, her eyes frankly revealing her hidden hungers. She was at this moment the living image of a man's desire, yet Troop made no move to touch her.

'Five minutes ago I was alone,' he said. 'The most alone I've ever been. There didn't seem to be a pleasant thing on the trail ahead. Not one. But now everything looks different to me. It looks good.'

'Because you're not alone?' Fern asked.

'Because you're here.' Then he asked soberly, 'Could you use a husband who's a fair-to-middling woodchopper, Fern?'

'You mean—we could stay on the Free Strip?' she asked, and when Troop nodded, she cried, 'Lew—oh, Lew!'

Troop leaned over then and took her in his arms. He said with exaggerated gravity, 'Monk Monroe once said that you were colder than icicles in a cave.'

'I'm not,' Fern whispered, snuggling close to him. 'I'm not cold with you.'

That was all the invitation a hungry drifter needed.

Photoset, printed and bound in Great Britain by
REDWOOD BURN LIMITED, Trowbridge, Wiltshire